"I've been watching you all evening, and you've been watching me, too."

Daniel lifted his hand to trace patterns on her jaw. "We've both been wondering how it would feel to be together again. Especially now that we're older, more experienced...confident in how to satisfy one another in bed. Come home with me, Lex. Let me peel that ridiculously sexy dress from your gorgeous body and replace it with my lips and hands. I'll make it good for you, I promise."

He'd make it too good and, yeah, that worried her. "Daniel, this is madness."

"So let's be mad, just for a night. In the morning we can go back to being a Clayton and a Slade, opposing forces in this long, futile war that we never started."

Alexis closed her eyes and shook her head. She wanted him but she didn't like wanting him, found herself wishing instead that she could put him in the past where he belonged. Maybe she did need to sleep with him again to flush him out of her system. After all, reality was never as good as fantasy, and then they could both finally move on.

Alexis leaned forward and stroked the pad of her thumb over his lower lip. "Take me to bed."

* * *

Lone Star Reunion by Joss Wood is part of the Texas Cattleman's Club: Bachelor Auction series.

Dear Reader,

Sometimes a book comes along that is pure sunshine and an absolute joy to write. For me, *Lone Star Reunion* is that book.

Over the course of the previous books in this installment of the Texas Cattleman's Club series, our lovely readers were introduced to Daniel and Alexis and their meddling, interfering but lovable grandparents, Gus and Rose. A fifty-year-old feud has kept Gus and Rose apart and played a part in Daniel and Alexis's breakup when they were teenagers. Now, a decade on, everyone is that much older. But not, unfortunately, wiser, and the road to true love is a rocky, dusty Texas trail!

Noticing Daniel and Alexis's attraction, Gus and Rose are determined to keep them apart, and conceive a plan to hold a charity bachelor auction in the hope that somebody else—anybody else—will catch their grandchildrens' attention! But fate is sneaky and the two octogenarians fall in love, grateful for a second chance.

Realizing that they were wrong to keep Daniel and Alexis apart, Gus and Rose hatch another plan, this one aimed at getting them together. What could possibly go wrong this time?

Happy reading,

Joss

Connect with me at www.josswoodbooks.com.

Twitter: @josswoodbooks

Facebook: Joss Wood Author

JOSS WOOD

———

LONE STAR REUNION

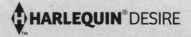

HARLEQUIN® DESIRE

Special thanks and acknowledgment are given
to Joss Wood for her contribution to the Texas
Cattleman's Club: Bachelor Auction series.

Recycling programs
for this product may
not exist in your area.

ISBN-13: 978-1-335-60343-2

Lone Star Reunion

Copyright © 2019 by Harlequin Books S.A.

Printed in U.S.A.

www.Harlequin.com

Joss Wood loves books and traveling—especially to the wild places of Southern Africa and, well, anywhere. She's a wife, a mom to two teenagers and slave to two cats. After a career in local economic development, she now writes full-time. Joss is a member of Romance Writers of America and Romance Writers of South Africa.

Books by Joss Wood

Harlequin Desire

The Ballantyne Billionaires

His Ex's Well-Kept Secret
One Night to Forever
The CEO's Nanny Affair
Little Secrets: Unexpectedly Pregnant

Love in Boston

Friendship on Fire
Hot Christmas Kisses
The Rival's Heir

Texas Cattleman's Club: Bachelor Auction

Lone Star Reunion

Visit her Author Profile page at Harlequin.com, or josswoodbooks.com, for more titles.

Don't miss a single book in the
Texas Cattleman's Club: Bachelor Auction
series!

Runaway Temptation
by *USA TODAY* bestselling author
Maureen Child

Most Eligible Texan
by *USA TODAY* bestselling author
Jules Bennett

Million Dollar Baby
by *USA TODAY* bestselling author
Janice Maynard

His Until Midnight
by Reese Ryan

The Rancher's Bargain
by Joanne Rock

Lone Star Reunion
by Joss Wood

Prologue

Over the decades many wedding receptions had been held at the Texas Cattleman's Club, and there had been a fair amount of scandals, for sure. Alexis Slade remembered talk of a groom being caught in a compromising position with the matron of honor, and a father of the groom passing out under a lavishly decorated bridal party table after streaking across the dance floor, wearing nothing more than a very lacy pink thong. There had been tearful brides, drunk brides, regretful brides and emotional brides, but Shelby Arthur was the first bride who hadn't made it to the altar.

The Goodman-Arthur wedding, or nonwedding, would undoubtedly be talked about for weeks on end. Alex looked across the still-crowded reception room and saw Reginald Goodman, father of the groom, with a tumbler of whiskey in his hand, looking pale but composed. Her eyes tracked left and there was the mother of the bride, a handkerchief clutched in her fist. Alex snorted at her wobbling lower lip, her crocodile tears. Daphne Goodman was a designer-dress-wearing barracuda who'd made no secret of the fact that she despised her son's fiancée and was totally against their marriage. Having been an object of Jared's affections in high school, Alex believed Shelby came to her senses just in time.

Marrying the spineless groom meant marrying his awful family—Brooke Goodman, Jared's sweet-natured sister, was the exception—and really, no woman deserved that. Marriage was tough enough without any added pressure from the in-laws. Jared and Shelby's marriage would've been a marriage of three, with Daphne Goodman calling the shots.

Alex turned when the door next to her right elbow opened and Rose Clayton walked into the reception area via the side entrance. Cool gray assessing eyes met hers and Alex reminded herself that she wasn't eighteen anymore, so the unofficial queen of the Texas Cattleman's Club should no longer intimidate her.

But she did.

Over that long summer ten years ago, Rose waged a war to separate her and Daniel, Rose's beloved grandson and heir. Gus, her own grandfather, had done the same. Because God and every Texan knew, family loyalty and a decades-old feud between Gus Slade and Rose Clayton trumped first love. At the time, she and Daniel had been the Romeo and Juliet of Royal, minus the death by poisoning.

Losing Daniel had felt like another death—she'd missed and mourned him that much. Alex remembered her tears, the desperation and loss she'd endured when Daniel refused to leave Royal with her so she could attend school out of state.

Daniel had said he belonged at The Silver C, but she disagreed, proclaiming they belonged together. They'd yelled; she'd cried. Daniel's stubbornness and intransigence, his unwillingness to choose her— *them*—ultimately killed their relationship.

Yes, they'd been young but, in his own unique way, he'd abandoned her. Unlike her parents, her childhood friend Gemma and, just last year, her beloved grandmother Sarah, Daniel had left her life through choice and not death.

And that somehow hurt more.

Rose approached her and a part of her still wanted to curl up in a ball when faced with Daniel's imperial grandmother. Annoyed with herself, Alex straightened her spine and managed a jerky nod. "Miss Rose."

"Alexis Slade."

Alex rolled her eyes when Rose turned her back on her and glided away, five foot something of sheer haughtiness and holier-than-thou poise. If not for their volatile history, she might even admire the woman for her steely self-assurance, her ability to carve out her rightful place in a world filled with take-charge alpha men.

But Rose was a Clayton and, as such, a sworn Slade enemy. Alex and her brother knew the basics of the Slade-Clayton feud: a half century ago, Gus, her grandfather, left Royal to make his fortune on the rodeo circuit, believing that Rose Clayton would wait for his return. He saved enough to buy a small spread next to the Clayton ranch and went to propose to Rose, excited to start his life with the woman he desperately loved. But Rose had married Ed the year before.

In doing so, Rose fired the first shot and war was declared.

Gus's marrying Rose's best friend—Alex's beloved grandmother Sarah—just escalated the conflict. And her grandfather buying up more portions of the once-mighty Clayton ranch was a nuclear strike. Families took their feuds seriously in Texas, and although sides were most certainly chosen, the Texas Cattleman's Club remained the demilitarized zone.

The Slades and Claytons, both old and young, were all members, and here within these walls, they had to play nice. Or when that wasn't feasible, they opted to ignore each other as much as possible. Just like Gus was ignoring Rose, and Alexis was ignoring Daniel, which was, annoyingly, very damn hard to do.

What woman with a pulse could? Surrendering to temptation, Alex looked toward the bar…and at the devastatingly handsome man who she'd once considered to be the love of her life. She drank in every inch of him. The black curls he hated—but she loved—and those mysterious dark brown eyes he'd inherited—everyone presumed—from his father, because his mother was light skinned with blue eyes. Boring brown, Daniel had once called them, but Alex vehemently disagreed. They could be as rich as expensive coffee, as deep as the night. However, they could also turn as hard as ship-destroying rocks on a jagged, inhospitable coastline.

So much had changed over the years, Alex mused with a wistful sigh. Her once-gangly boyfriend was now taller, broader, every inch a man. He was still lean but with hard muscles and a harder streak. Strong stubble covered his jaw and he looked as good in a tuxedo as he did in worn jeans, but neither was his sexiest look.

A naked Daniel Clayton, as she'd discovered when she was younger, could easily be classified as one of the wonders of the world.

In the past decade, her ex had done quite well for himself. He'd acquired degrees in both agriculture and business, and all the hard work he put into The Silver C had, judging by his designer tuxedo and the German sports car he occasionally drove, paid off. He was smart, wealthy and good-looking, and that trifecta made him one of the most sought-after bachelors in the area. Hell, possibly even the state. Although he hadn't brought a date to this wedding, Daniel Clayton was never, so she'd heard, short of a female companion.

In bed or out of it.

A hand on her arm pulled her eyes off her former lover and she smiled at Rachel Kincaid, her closest friend. Alex didn't make friends easily, but Rachel was someone who'd sneaked under her defenses.

"Why are you standing here by yourself?" her friend asked, handing her a glass of champagne.

"Trying to avoid another conversation about Shelby or what I think of the new president of the TCC," Alex admitted, taking the glass with a grateful smile.

"James Harris is a great guy."

Alex nodded. "I like him, too." She glanced at the tall African American man standing next to the right of them, talking to Rose Clayton. "And, oh my God, he's seriously hot."

In fact, there were many drop-dead gorgeous men in this room, most of them members of the TCC. She knew why she was single—chronic commitment and abandonment issues—but that didn't mean she had to be celibate. Yet she was.

"You keep looking at Daniel Clayton," Rachel remarked. "Not that I blame you. I swear he was birthed by an angel."

An unfortunate choice of words, Alex thought wryly, since Daniel's mom was reputed to be anything but celestial. Daniel never spoke about Stephanie but there were enough gossips in Royal to ascertain a little of what his life with his tempestuous and unstable mother had been like. According to the grapevine, Rose had been the only responsible adult in his life. His loyalty to his grandmother was rock-solid and unshakable.

Their romance had been doomed from the start. Because, as it turned out, Alex had never been able to compete with Rose and Daniel's fierce allegiance to The Silver C ranch.

"Matt Galloway is just as good-looking," Alex commented, partly to be perverse but also to distract Rachel from linking her and Daniel together. There was no "her and Daniel," and there hadn't been in a long, long time. And she wasn't lying, Matt Galloway was a young Clooney: as good-looking, as rich and charming, and as much of a reputed playboy as George used to be.

"He is—was—Billy's best friend." Alex wasn't sure what Matt's looks had to do with him being Rachel's dead husband's friend, but she was familiar with the don't-go-there look on Rachel's face, since it was an expression she often used. Alex liked her own privacy, so she didn't push Rachel.

Rachel wound her arm around Alex's waist and squeezed. "Have I said thank you lately for letting me stay with you at the Lone Wolf Ranch?"

"We love having you and baby Ellie there," Alex responded.

"And I don't take it personally that you frequently run away to Sarah's tree house."

"That's more to avoid Gus's lectures about finding a husband and giving him a great-grandchild than avoiding you, as you well know. Gus is determined to get me bound and breeding. I, on the other hand, need to think about getting back to Houston, to my life there. I came home to be with Grandma Sarah in her last days, but I'm still here, a year after her death. Royal was only meant to be a stopgap. My life isn't here."

"Sure looks like it is," Rachel commented. "As a digital-media strategist, you can work anywhere in the world, and you love the ranch, spending time with Gus."

Of course she did, but being with Gus and working part-time as the Lone Wolf's business manager didn't stop her from missing her grandmother with an intensity that still threatened to drop her to her knees. It didn't stop her from wallowing in the past, from remembering how happy she and Daniel had once been before she learned that love didn't conquer all.

Alex sucked in her breath when his eyes slammed into hers and, as always, she felt caressed by the light of a million stars. Electric tingles skittered across her skin, tightened her nipples, sent heat to that place between her legs. This was just red-hot, carnal lust, and nothing, she silently insisted, like what they'd experienced so long ago.

Back then, they'd been constantly drunk. On love, on each other. They'd hurtled headfirst into love and sex and passion, blithely thinking they could handle the thousand-degree fire they'd created, stoked and fed.

Pfft. She'd emerged with third-degree burns. But the worst part? Alex still found Daniel physically intoxicating. And judging by the unbanked desire flashing in his eyes, she made him feel equally off balance.

Good. He deserved nothing less.

Rachel accepted a dance from Gus, old flirt that he was, and Alex, wanting fresh air, slipped out the side door. She inhaled the cool, fragrant night air and wrapped her arms around her waist as she walked toward the gardens surrounding the TCC. In daylight it was immediately apparent that the surrounding grounds, flower beds and paths that meandered through the once-glorious garden needed some updating and attention. But at night the gardens were mysterious and welcoming, an old friend. She remembered playing hide-and-seek in these gardens with her brother and her friends, sneaking down to the small pond to steal a kiss from Daniel Clayton, away from their eagle-eyed grandparents.

Fun times, Alex thought with a bittersweet pang.

She heard the crunch of boots on the gravel path, and then a jacket covered her bare shoulders. She inhaled his familiar scent—sandalwood and leather, wood and wildness. Big, manly hands settled on her shoulders and she instinctively leaned back, her head resting against his collarbone, his warm breath on her ear.

Suddenly she was eighteen again. Daniel had his hands on her…and all was right with her world.

"Lexi." Daniel's deep voice rumbled over her skin, as deep and dark as the night.

Alex knew that she should run away. But she was so tired of tamping down her fantasies of what it would be like to have Daniel naked and in her bed. Of dreaming how he would make love. Teenage Daniel had been hesitant, cautious, but adult Daniel would possess her the same way he did everything else, with confidence and raw virility.

And she wanted him. God, how she wanted him!

Alex sighed as his hand brazenly moved over her shoulder, down her chest, to slide under the lapel of his jacket and cup her breast. His thumb swiped her nipple as he pulled her earlobe between his teeth, gently nibbling.

"Still so sexy, Lexi. Love what you are wearing."

She couldn't remember what she'd put on so she glanced down… Right, a loose, off-the-shoulder black top with a full, flower-patterned pale pink skirt.

Alex knew she should push him away, but instead of being sensible, she placed her hand behind her back, her fingers seeking out his erection. There it was, hard and long and thick, and she heard his low, guttural moan as his cock jerked beneath her touch. Then she was making whimpering sounds of her own as his hand pushed aside the fabric of her top so that he could feel her naked flesh and pull her tight nipple between his fingers.

She lifted her head up and to the side, and then his mouth was on hers. Parting her lips to receive his tongue, she moaned her frustration when he smiled against her mouth, silently telling her that he enjoyed teasing her, making her wait. He'd always been more patient, more interested in drawing out every moment of their pleasure.

Daniel's chaste kisses were in direct contrast to his roaming hands. He bunched the fabric of her skirt and pulled it up her legs, and his fingers trailed up her thighs, played with the tiny V shape of her panties. Alex felt him shudder when he discovered her panties were only comprised of one triangle and a few thin cords.

"Naughty underwear, Miss Slade," Daniel growled against her mouth.

"Shut up and touch me, Clayton," Alex demanded, spinning around and slapping her hands on his cotton-covered chest. Ignoring his loose tie and open collar, she gripped his shirt and yanked it from his pants, desperate to find hot, sexy, olive-toned skin. Her fingers danced across a set of impressive washboard abs, and she pushed her fingers between that hard stomach and the band of his pants, seeking and finding the tip of his erection. Daniel released a low hiss, sucked in his stomach and suddenly she had more of him against her fingers, hot and oh-so potent.

"I want you, Lex," Daniel muttered, smacking her bare butt cheek and pulling her into him, squashing her hand between her body and his erection. Needing more, needing everything—she'd missed him, missed this so much—Alex lifted her thigh and wrapped it over his hip, grateful to yoga for making her supple. Then nothing but fabric separated her core from his shaft, and she rocked her hips and lifted her mouth up to his to be kissed.

This time he didn't hold back and his tongue swept between her parted lips, branding, rediscovering, wiping away any doubts that reliving the past was foolish and dangerous.

There was only Daniel, his taste and heat and power, the adult version of the boy she'd known so long ago. Standing in his arms, panting and with soaked panties, her only thoughts were of how much she'd missed his touch, missed his kisses. In this moment they didn't have feuding grandparents, unforgivable betrayals or hurt and pain between them. There was only desire—hot, potent and demanding.

Daniel wrenched his mouth off hers, and in the moonlight his eyes, normally so shuttered, were as deep and dark as a desert night. "Come home with me, Lex."

She had to be rational…and she couldn't be, not when she had her hand in his pants. She couldn't think, breathe. Alex pulled her hand from between their bodies and tried to step back, but Daniel's hands on her hips kept her up close and very personal. "Dan, don't ask me that."

"Why? Because you are scared you're going to say yes?"

It was a typical no-frills Daniel response. He never beat around the bush, and although he was the strong and silent type, when he did speak, people listened. Her ex just had a way of cutting through BS to get to the heart of the matter, and as per usual, he was right. She was terrified that she was going to say yes, but even more scared that she was going to force herself to say no.

"I've been watching you all evening and you've been watching me, too," Daniel murmured, lifting his hand to trace patterns on her jaw. "We've both been wondering what it would feel like to be together again. Especially now that we're older, more experienced... confident in how to satisfy one another in bed."

She was sexually confident? Oh, she was anything but. She might be older and wiser, but she was still more girl next door than femme fatale.

"Come home with me, Lex. Let me peel that ridiculously sexy dress from your gorgeous body and replace it with my lips and hands. I'll make it good for you, I promise."

He'd make it *too* good, and yeah, that worried her. "Daniel, this is *madness*."

"So let's be mad, just for a night. In the morning we

can go back to being a Clayton and a Slade, opposing forces in this long, futile war that we never started."

Alex closed her eyes and shook her head. She wanted him but she didn't like wanting him, found herself wishing instead that she could put him in the past, where he belonged. Maybe she *did* need to sleep with him again to flush him out of her system. After all, reality was never as good as fantasy, and then they could both finally move on.

"So, yes or no?"

Alex thought she saw apprehension in his eyes, the fear that she'd reject him, but the emotions flashed across his features too quickly for her to be sure. "Yeah, I'm coming with you."

Daniel stared down at her, his handsome face serious. "Your place or mine?"

Alex thought about their options, knowing that the ranch house at the Lone Wolf was out of the question and, as she'd heard, Daniel had converted an old barn on The Silver C. While his house was a better option than Gus's mansion—Daniel might be met with the working end of her grandpa's shotgun if they were caught—their chances of discovery were still too high.

Which left only one other place available to them…

"Sarah's tree house."

Daniel's hand tightened on her hip and she knew that he was remembering, just as she was.

A long time ago, the tree house had been a boys' fort and a girls' secret club. It had held sleep outs and camping trips and overnight sleepovers. Much later it had been the place where Daniel took her virginity, where they'd spent stolen afternoons and blissful starry nights.

"You remember where it is, right?"

Daniel rubbed his jaw. "Of course I can find it. I just haven't been there since…"

You left, Alex filled in the words for him. The tree house was deep in Slade land and Daniel had no reason or wish to be on Slade land. Land that had once been part of The Silver C spread.

The river-fronted land was one of the first parcels of land Gus bought from Rose when times had got tough, and Alex knew that Daniel mourned the loss of the property. The Silver C had once been the largest spread in four counties, but it was now on par with the Lone Wolf in acreage, a bit of a comedown for the once-mighty Claytons.

"I'll meet you at the tree house," Daniel said, his voice clipped. He lifted his wrist to look at his expensive watch. "In half an hour?" He rubbed his hand over his jaw and shook his head. "I can't believe that I am risking getting splinters in my butt to have you again. Nobody but you, Alex Slade, would tempt me to do this…"

His words shouldn't make her smile but they did. She opened her mouth to explain that the tree house wasn't as bad as it had been… No, she'd let it be a surprise.

"Are you going to walk there?" Daniel asked.

In moonlight or bright sunshine, she always walked to the tree house. "Yes."

"I'm going to go home, pick up my dirt bike and I'll be there as soon as I can," Daniel told her, his eyes steady on her face.

Good, that gave her some time to think about what she was doing, to talk herself out of this madness.

Daniel narrowed his gaze. "Do *not* stand me up, Alexis."

Although it unnerved her how he'd been able to read her thoughts, she couldn't suppress the shiver of excitement that tap-danced up and down her spine. He was gorgeous and determined and he wanted her.

No, she wouldn't stand him up. She couldn't; she wanted this, wanted *him*. "I'll be there."

Daniel nodded, swiped his mouth across hers in a brief but molten-lava-hot kiss. "See that you are."

One

Mid-November

Daniel Clayton released a low curse and buried his head in the soft pillow, cursing his early-morning alarm. Unfortunately, neither cattle nor his ranch hands cared that he'd spent most of the night making love, that he'd had minimal sleep. The Silver C Ranch and his grandmother demanded a daily pound of flesh and since he didn't tolerate excuses or less than 100 percent effort, he knew he should haul his ass out of bed and get to it. He rolled over and pressed his chest to Lexi's back, filling his hand with her perfect, perfect breast. Daniel skimmed his thumb across her nipple and buried his nose in her fragrant hair. Best way to wake up, bar none. His rock-hard erection pushed into her bottom and he skated his hand down her torso, across her stomach, and his fingers flirted with the V shape below. There was nothing like sleepy, lazy sex… His cell phone alarm screeched again.

"Dammit, Clayton," Lex muttered, reaching across him to grab his phone. Mercifully, the strident alarm ceased, and despite wanting Lexi again, Daniel found himself drifting back to sleep. Then Alex's sharp elbow dug into his ribs and he rolled over, frowning.

"What was that for?"

"Sun's up in forty-five minutes, and we both have to leave," Alex told him, whipping off the covers and exposing his naked body to the chilly morning air.

The tree house was heated by a woodstove, which they didn't bother to light because a stream of smoke from the chimney would raise questions—questions neither of them wanted to answer. As it was, he'd already endured a few lectures from Rose, demanding to know the status of his love life. He'd blown her off, as usual, but then she'd upped the ante by expressing her fervent hope that he'd meet a lovely girl through the upcoming bachelor auction—as if!—and that she would be bitterly disappointed if she found out that he was carrying on with "that Slade girl."

Since that Slade girl was currently standing naked by the window, long blond hair tumbling down her oh-so-sexy back, he didn't give a rat's ass what his grandmother or anyone else thought. They'd been hooking up for six weeks—maybe a week or so more—and he'd enjoyed every second he'd spent with Alex. But what they shared was sex and desire and heat and want and nothing his grandmother needed to worry about.

He loved his grandmother—he did—but he just wished she'd stay out of his damn business. Alex, what they had together, was separate from The Silver C— one didn't impact the other. For a decade his entire focus had been on the family spread, trying to restore the somewhat tarnished reputation of the Clayton clan. While Rose held the respect of the residents of the town of Royal and the counties of Maverick and Colonial, his late grandfather, Ed, and his mother, Stephanie, did not. One was a bastard and the other was irresponsible, wild and borderline psycho. Despite his dubious parentage, he'd worked hard to command a little of the respect his grandmother did.

And he thought he was getting there.

While not nearly as big as it had been in its heyday, The Silver C was now regarded as being one of the best-managed spreads in the country, lauded for its breeding program and producing award-winning bulls. He had a waiting list as long as his arm for buyers wanting to purchase his quarter horses, and he ran the entire ranching operation with the utmost professionalism and integrity. And by doing so, he'd recently been inducted as a member of the Texas Cattleman's Club.

Daniel sat up, rested his forearms on his thighs and shoved his hands through his hair before running his palm over his stubble-covered jaw. He watched as Alex picked up a sweatshirt—one of his—and frowned when the voluminous fabric covered her to midthigh. She then pulled her hair out from under the band of the garment and gathered it into a messy knot on top of her head, and he thought that he'd never seen anyone so naturally beautiful, so effortlessly sexy.

"I'm going to make coffee. Do you have time for a cup?"

Daniel glanced at his watch and nodded. "Yeah, I do. Thanks."

He watched Alex leave the room, her hips swaying seductively as she did so. She'd been pretty as a teenager but she was spectacular as a grown woman. Blue eyes the color of the summer sky, high cheekbones and that luscious, made-to-kiss mouth. Yards and yards of fragrant, wavy hair. And... God, that body...lean and slender, finely boned but with curves and dips and flares that made his mouth water.

At eighteen he'd thought he'd loved her, but now, ten years later, he knew that he'd been blinded by lust, had confused love with desire. He didn't believe in romantic love and Daniel sometimes wondered if he ever, deep down, really had. God knew he hadn't been exposed to any marital, or even family, harmony growing up.

He was the unwanted son of Rose's daughter, who had also been raised in a tense household. There had been little love between Rose and his maternal grandfather, and his mother, Stephanie, wasn't able to love anyone but herself. He'd been the unwanted result of one of Stephanie's many bad decisions when it came to men.

Daniel had no idea who his father was and one of Stephanie's favorite games had been to play "Who's Your Daddy?" She'd thrown out names to tease, later telling him that she'd made up names and oc- cupations to amuse herself. It was cold comfort that Stephanie had also played Rose like a fiddle, using him as her bow.

Thanks to his dysfunctional childhood, he was cynical about love. But he did believe in family, in loyalty, in hard work and respect—Rose had shown him the value of those traits, in both word and deed. She'd never lied to him, not even during those worst times, when Stephanie was crazier than a wet hen.

So when his grandmother expressed her reserva- tions about his teenage romance with Alex, calmly pointing out that he'd be throwing away his future at the ranch to follow a girl he *thought* he might love, he'd eventually listened to her advice. And why wouldn't he? She was the one stable adult in his life, the only person he'd ever felt was looking after his best interests.

And yeah, after emotionally and physically di- vorcing himself from his mother, he vowed that he'd never let anyone emotionally blackmail him again.

Shaking off his disturbing thoughts, Daniel stood up, strode to the small bathroom next to the only bedroom and used the facilities. He returned to the master suite, smiling as he remembered how surprised he'd been when he'd first laid eyes on this renovated tree house.

Gone was the rickety structure from before. Now a sleek, beautifully designed house rested in the massive cypress trees overlooking the river that meandered its way through both The Silver C and the Lone Wolf ranches. Instead of a one-room platform, the tree house consisted of a master bedroom, a sleeping loft above the main living space, this tiny bathroom and a small kitchenette. The abundance of windows and a sliding glass wall allowed for amazing views of the river and Lone Wolf land. He wished he could lie on the sprawling deck, beer in his hand, Stetson over his face, soaking up some winter rays. But there was work to do, and the needs of The Silver C Ranch always came first.

Hearing Alex walking up the stairs to the bedroom, he stepped into his jeans and pulled on his shirt, then his fleece-lined leather jacket. Sitting down on the edge of the bed, he reached for his socks and boots, lifting his head as Alex appeared in the doorway. He took the cup of coffee she held out—hot and black— and sipped gratefully. Another three of these and he might feel vaguely human.

She sat down on the bed next to him, scooted backward and crossed her legs. "Dan…"

There was something odd in the way she said his name, so he whipped his head around to look at her, his eyes narrowing at the frown pulling her arched eyebrows together. "Yeah?"

Alex cradled her mug in both hands and he saw the tremble in her fingers, the way the rim of the cup vibrated. Oh crap, this wasn't good. He removed the cup from her fingers, placed it on the wooden bedside table and turned back to face her. "What's wrong, Lex?"

"Has Rose been giving you grief about me?"

He really didn't want to have this conversation now, didn't have the time for it. "Yeah. She asked me whether we were seeing each other, told me that she wouldn't be happy if I was."

Alex sighed. "I got a similar lecture from Gus, telling me how it would break his heart if he found out we were together." Alex looked miserable and Daniel could relate. Neither of them liked disappointing their grandparents.

"Gus is trying to set me up with guys who are taking part in the bachelor auction."

"That damned auction," Daniel growled, the thought of being sold like a steer raising his blood pressure. Then, to add insult to injury, he would have to pay for the date with the woman who'd paid to spend time with him. Why couldn't he just write a check to cover the costs of the date? Hell, he'd double, even triple, the amount if he could get out of going on a stupid date with someone not of his choosing.

"That *damned* auction is going to raise an awesome amount of money for the Pancreatic Cancer

Foundation." Daniel saw the blue fire in Alex's eyes and reminded himself that the charity auction was her pet project. Her beloved grandmother Sarah had died from the disease, and as it was a cause that was near and dear to her heart, Lex had committed herself to raising funds to find a cure.

"I'll be glad when it's over," Alex said. "A few more sleeps and counting. Roll on Saturday and then Gus can stop throwing me into the arms of any man with a pulse."

The thought of Alexis being in another man's arms was enough to have him grinding his teeth together. Daniel reminded himself that he had no right to feel jealous, but the enamel still flew off his teeth. Reaching across him to pick up her cup of coffee, her hair brushed his face and he inhaled her lavender-and-wildflower scent. He immediately felt himself grow hard, and as much as it pained him, he told himself to stand down.

"If I don't leave soon, Lex, I'm going to be late. What's on your mind?"

Alex sipped, sighed and sipped again, before finally getting to the point. "I…um…think we should put this on hold, at least for a while."

"*This* meaning us?"

Alex nodded. "I've got a lot on my mind, so much to do, and while this has been fun, it's taking time and energy I don't currently have."

Daniel felt the prick—hell, stab!—of dismay and pushed the pain away. Sure, he hadn't expected this to last forever, but damn, he and Lex were good together. They enjoyed each other, knew exactly how to make each other writhe and squirm and scream. It would be a good long while, Daniel admitted, before he could even *think* about sleeping with someone else.

Because Alexis—warm and wonderful—was truly one of a kind.

Alex looked like she was waiting for an answer, so he shrugged and uttered the only word he could wrap his tongue around. "Okay."

Disappointment flashed in her eyes. At his one-syllable answer or because he wasn't arguing for them to carry on?

"I'd also like to tell our grandparents that we are wise to them trying to set us up with other people, that they can't interfere in our love lives," Alex stated, her voice determined.

"You want to tackle them together? In the same room?" Daniel heard the skepticism in his voice. "Would Royal survive the fallout?"

"I think it would have more impact," Alex stubbornly replied.

"They've avoided each other for five decades, Lex. You're not going to get them in the same room, at the same time." This feud was exhausting but it wasn't theirs to fight. Gus and Rose had decades of tumultuous history to work through, and Daniel wasn't fool enough to get sucked up in that craziness.

Besides, he had bigger things to deal with, like

Alex cutting him off. He didn't want this to end…
"You sure this is what you want to do, Lex?"

Alex lifted her shoulders, dropped them and released a long-suffering sigh. "I'm tired of the lectures, the disapproving looks from Gus. I'm tired
of sneaking around. I need more sleep and I have a
couple of personal decisions I need to make. You're
a…complication."

A complication, huh? "It's just sex, Alex."

Was that reminder directed at her or himself?

Annoyance glimmered in Lexi's gorgeous blue
eyes. "Of course it is, but since it's sapping my time
and energy, it needs to stop." She looked away from
him, shrugged before dragging her eyes back to his.
"Maybe once the auction is over, after the holidays,
if I'm around, we could maybe pick things up again."

So many maybes, Daniel thought, pulling on his
boot. *Wait, what did she say?* "You said, *if* you're
around? Are you thinking of leaving?"

Another thought to cool his head. He definitely
wasn't getting enough sleep!

"I've had a job offer that might take me back to
Houston," Alex said. "I've stayed in Royal longer
than I thought I would. My plan was always to return there."

"What's the offer?" Daniel asked, standing up and
tucking his shirt into his jeans.

"Managing partner in a social media strategy
firm. It's a good offer. I've always wanted to be my
own boss."

He quirked a brow. "Isn't that what you are here on the ranch?"

"Gus is still the boss, Dan," she reminded him. "And while I can run the finances, I'm not a rancher. In Royal, everything has a memory associated with it. My parents, Sarah…"

He heard her unsaid *you* and could almost taste the emotion in her voice. They'd both had hard childhoods, had been knocked around by life, but he knew that losing her parents as a little girl had rocked her world. And then to lose Sarah, on top of all that, had truly devastated her. "I am sorry, Lex. Sorry for you, for Gus."

Alex managed a wobbly smile. "Thanks, I appreciate it." Standing up, she placed her hand on his chest, and Daniel felt his heart rate kick up, his throat tightening. Alex just had to touch him and the thoughts of stripping their clothes off and taking her again were front and center. He forcibly held himself still as Alex stood up on her pretty painted toes to kiss the side of his mouth. "Thanks for this, Dan. It was fun. And maybe it exorcised some ghosts."

Yeah, but maybe it also, Daniel couldn't help thinking, *created a whole bunch more*.

She'd said goodbye to him as a teenager but watching him walk away as an adult was surprisingly a great deal harder than she'd imagined it would be. She'd been madly in love with him then, but she wasn't in love with him now, so… Why on earth was she so upset?

You have to let him go. There is no other option. This is not a situation where you can have the cowboy and ride him, as well.

But she still couldn't keep her eyes off him as he strode toward his dirt bike. Sighing appreciatively, she watched as he threw a long, muscular leg over the saddle and gripped the handlebars, dark curls shining in the early-morning light. Man, he was gorgeous, a perfect combination of Anglo and Hispanic. Olive skin, black hair, those smoldering brown eyes and that lean, powerful physique.

Alex leaned her forearms on the railing of the deck and watched her lover—no, her *ex-lover*—ride away, ignoring her wildly beating heart. There was no denying that this man had the ability to liquefy her insides, to shut down her thought processes, to invade her thoughts. But he'd also broken her heart, and she'd never give him the power to do that again.

She'd noticed that Daniel was starting to sneak under her skin, that her thoughts went to him at inopportune times—like every ten seconds—and this morning, while making coffee, she'd thought about asking him whether he wanted to attend a country music concert in Joplin with her the following week. They could stay in a bed-and-breakfast, try out that new restaurant she'd heard was fabulous…

Shocked at her thoughts, she'd given herself a mental slap. Daniel wasn't someone to make plans around, to date, to spend time with. If she was starting to think of him as a potential partner and not just as a fun, sexy hookup, then it was time to cut him loose.

So she did.

When the sound of Dan's bike faded away, Alex walked back into the bedroom and sat on the edge of the bed, staring at the expensive Persian carpet beneath her feet. *Only in Texas would you find an exquisite Persian carpet on the floor of a very up-scale tree house*, Alex thought. Only her grandmother Sarah would put it there. Damn, she still missed her. But Sarah, like her parents, was gone, and Alex couldn't help feeling that the people who loved her the most tended to leave her...

Intellectually, Alex understood that death was a part of life, that people died and hearts got broken. Tough times came along to make one stronger, that everything was a lesson...blah, blah, blah.

But losing her parents and her beloved grandmother long before they were supposed to go was just damn unfair. It was like some bored god was using her heart as a football.

Daniel had left her, too, but his desertion had strangely hurt the most. It was his choice to leave her and it was obvious, even so many years later, that she'd loved Daniel so much more than he loved her...

Alex flopped back onto the bed and placed her arm over her eyes. And that was why she'd cut him loose today: she couldn't—wouldn't—put herself in the position of being left brokenhearted again.

Wanting to stop wallowing, she started to make a mental list of everything she had to do today. Getting together with Rachel to plan Tessa's makeover was high on her list. As the only bachelorette up for auction, they were going to make her the star of the show. Not that Tess needed much help—the girl was stunningly beautiful, both inside and out.

And as the master of the ceremonies, she had to plan her introductions, find some funny jokes to keep the audience entertained. She also had to psych herself into selling Daniel, the only man she'd seen naked in the longest time, to some woman with a healthy bank account. That was going to be so much fun.

Not.

Alex felt nausea climb up her throat. Really, she was being ridiculous, having a physical reaction to auctioning off Daniel. Yes, sure, the idea of sending her former flame off on a date with another woman wasn't a pleasant prospect, but they'd just shared their bodies, not their hearts and souls. She had no hold on him—she didn't *want* a damned hold on him, and that was why she'd severed their connection! She was being utterly asinine by allowing her emotions to rule her head, and this behavior was unworthy of a Slade.

But still, the nausea wouldn't subside and Alex cursed herself as she bolted for the bathroom and made her acquaintance with the toilet bowl.

Two

Alex stared down at the long list attached to her clipboard, wondering if she would survive this crazy day. And what had she been thinking, agreeing to be the emcee for The Great Royal Bachelor Auction? It was one thing being the master—mistress?—of ceremonies at friends' weddings and birthday parties, but this auction was a major social event.

What she'd thought would be a small local fundraiser had morphed into something a great deal bigger and was attracting press attention from media outlets in both Austin and Dallas. The tickets to the function had sold out within a day or two, but the loud demands from wealthy single women from the two cities and the neighboring town of Joplin forced her and Rachel to upscale the event, adding another five tables to the already crowded TCC function room.

Who would've thought that this small-town auction for their eligible bachelors would've generated so much buzz? Alex flicked through the program, looking at the faces of her bachelors and lone bachelorette. Who was she kidding? If was the perfect opportunity for wealthy singles with money to burn to buy themselves a hot date. Good, because she intended to make them pay mightily for the privilege.

Alex glanced at her watch, saw that it was just past four and looked down at her messy list. The tables were set, and the flower arrangements had arrived and looked superb. The band was doing a sound check and she heard the haunting sounds of a saxophone drifting from the ballroom to this anteroom that would host the bachelors as they were waiting for their turns to be auctioned. Alex walked over to the fridge, yanked open the door and was relieved to see the bottles of beer that would be needed to calm nervous dispositions. She smiled. Her bachelors were successful businessmen, alpha men every one of them, but every time they were reminded that they'd have to stand in the spotlight and be auctioned off like prize bulls, they all looked terrified.

Hearing the door to the greenroom open, she shut the fridge door and turned to see waiters from the Royal Diner entering the room, carrying platters of food. As she well knew, nothing short of a nuclear holocaust would stop her cowboys from eating.

"Hey, guys." Alex indicated the table where she wanted the platters to be placed. "Those look amazing. What did Amanda send over?"

"The Royal Diner's famous ribs, sliders, quiches. Doughnut and choc chip cookies for dessert."

"Please thank Amanda again for her generous donation. The guys and Tessa will appreciate it." Alex dug in her pocket to pull out a tip. She waved away their thanks, and when she was alone, she placed her clipboard between two of the platters and ran through her list again.

Flowers. Check.

Band. Check.

Food. Check.

Test sound system. That was currently happening.

Tessa's makeover. Alex checked her watch again. She'd allocated forty-five minutes for her and Rachel to give Tessa a makeover. Well, to be honest, to hold Tess's hand while the professionals she and Rachel hired did Tess's hair and makeup. Tess was going to rock the house tonight. Alex smiled. Girl power was a marvelous thing.

Tess reminded Alex of Gemma—she was as humble, as sweet and unaware of her good looks as Gemma had been. Alex pushed her fist into her sternum, thinking of her redheaded, emerald-eyed friend, a band of freckles across her nose. Sixteen years had passed since Gemma's death, but there were times, just like today, when she felt that Gemma was just waiting for her to call, like she was around the corner, about to stride back into her life.

She still missed her best friend; sometimes it felt like she'd lost her a few weeks back instead of so long ago. But grief, as she learned, had no respect for time. She'd lost her parents at ten, her best friend at twelve and Sarah just a year ago. She remembered her parents as well as she did Sarah. And Gemma as well as she remembered Sarah.

She'd heard that memories fade, that lost ones become indistinct. It had yet to happen to her. She could be doing something mundane and she'd hear Gemma's laugh, Sarah's voice or smell her mom's scent, and grief would slam into her, stopping her in her tracks.

When the pain subsided, just a little, she was left feeling abandoned, so damn alone. She was able to wrangle grief back into its cage, but those other feelings always lingered, casually snacking on her soul.

Could anyone blame her for pushing people away? She loved hard and she loved deep, giving all that she had. Sometime in the future, hopefully a long time from now, she'd have to face losing her grandfather Gus. Losing him, she hoped, would be easier than losing her parents, Gemma and Sarah. They'd all died way before their times, but hopefully her healthy and fit grandfather would live until he was a hundred and slip off in his sleep after a life well lived. She could live with that—it was the circle of life—and unlike before, she wouldn't feel abandoned.

Alex flipped the program over and traced Daniel's gorgeous face with the tip of her finger. Although she was right to put some distance between them, she still ached for him for him with every fiber of her being. Warmth pooled through her as she remembered the way he kissed her, the way his clever hands would stroke her body, the rasp of his stubble, the play of hard muscles under her hands.

The growl of his voice against her mouth, painting her skin with sinfully sexy words...

Tonight is all about making you weep as I pleasure you...

Just feeling your eyes on me makes me so hard.
You're going to pass out from satisfaction...

Daniel was a master of the art of talking dirty, using words and phrases that upped the sexy factor by 1000 percent. Then he lived up to his words with his skillful touch and used his mouth like a Jedi Master.

She missed him...

No, her body missed him. Her body missed him a whole bunch...

But stepping away from Daniel had been a wise move and one she'd make again. Her self-protection instinct had been carefully, meticulously honed and was now scalpel sharp. Nobody would slice and dice her again.

Alex shoved the program under the rest of her papers and straightened. Returning to her list, she lifted the plastic cover off the nearest platter and reached for a doughnut. She groaned as the treat touched her tongue, sighing at the prefect combination of fat and sugar.

God, so good. Alex chewed, swallowed and chewed again, polishing off the doughnut in three bites. She reached for another and it was halfway to her mouth when she heard a horrified gasp from the doorway.

"What the hell are you doing, Slade?" Rachel demanded, hands on her slim hips, brown eyes narrowed.

Alex pulled off a piece and chewed. Swallowing, she lifted her eyebrows at the astonished look on Rachel's face. What was her problem? "Um, eating a doughnut? Freshly made, courtesy of Amanda Battle."

"Actually, Jillian from the pie shop made them, but that's neither here nor there." Rachel stepped into the room and closed the door behind her. "Why are you eating them?"

Was that a trick question? "Because they are good?"

Rachel scratched her forehead, still looking confused. "Alex, I haven't seen you eat sugar in four years. You don't eat junk food, *ever.*"

Alex looked at the doughnut in her hand, puzzled. Rachel was right, she never ate junk food and very infrequently ate carbs. So why on earth was she eating one now? And, knowing that, why was she unable to throw it in the trash?

Alex popped the last of the doughnut into her

mouth and contemplated her actions. Was she finally losing it? Was the stress of organizing the bachelor auction, breaking up with Daniel and trying to work through the job offer she'd had from Houston finally getting to her?

"Alex, are you okay?"

"It's just a doughnut, Rach. Okay, two little doughnuts," Alex retorted. Then she reached for a paper napkin and wiped the powdered sugar off her fingers. "My sugar levels are probably low. I just needed a boost."

"I'd believe that if I didn't see the way you refused coffee this morning, wrinkling your nose at the smell. And last night you drank some chamomile tea."

"I had indigestion."

"You loathe chamomile tea," Rachel pointed out.

Was her best friend trying to make a point? Because if she was, she was taking a hell of a long time to get to it. "You've obviously got something to say, Rachel, so why don't you spit it out so I can get back to work?"

"Ooh, grumpy," Rachel quipped, stepping forward to grip Alex's biceps with her hands. "Honey, I think you are pregnant."

Alex had never thought it possible that she could feel like she was burning up from the inside, as well as feeling soul-deep cold. "Okay, that's simply not funny."

"Am I laughing?" Rachel asked, her expression serious. "Alex, having been through this myself, I can spot a pregnancy at fifty paces. You, my friend, are pregnant."

"Stop saying that!" Alex hissed, panic closing her throat. "I can't be! I had my period…"

Rachel lifted her eyebrows, patiently waiting for an answer.

"Give me a sec, dammit! I have to think!" Alex pulled her phone from the back pocket of her jeans and clicked on her calendar app. She always kept a record of her cycle and she'd show Rachel that she was talking out of her hat. Alex flipped through dates, didn't see anything and flipped back a month. Oh man, there was no denying it. She was late.

"Apart from eating junk food, has anything else changed? Have you felt nauseous, tired?"

"I threw up a couple of weeks back, felt nauseous once last week and I'm tired because I've been organizing this damn function. I can't be pregnant… Maybe I have a bug! It's far too early for me to have any symptoms of pregnancy anyway."

That was the answer, she had a bug, had picked up a virus. Phew!

"It's not a disease, Alex," Rachel patiently replied. "And everyone is different."

"Oh God. Oh God."

Rachel's grip on her arms tightened. "Breathe, honey. Let's think about this logically. Did Daniel use condoms? Are you on birth control?"

"You know I've been seeing Daniel?" Alex demanded. "Who else knows? Does Gus? Oh crap!"

"It was a guess, which you just confirmed," Rachel replied, her voice low and smooth. "So, condoms?"

"Yes, dammit. We are responsible adults who don't make juvenile errors." Alex bent over, covered her face with her hands and dropped to her haunches. "But there was one time…he pulled out and then put on a condom. God! No! I can't be pregnant, Rach. I can't!"

"I think there's a good possibility that you are." Rachel ran a gentle hand over Alex's hair. "Alex, just breathe. In and out. Good girl."

Alex sucked in air, using every bit of self-control she had to push away the breath-stealing panic that threatened to engulf her. Still on her haunches, she placed her hand on the floor to steady herself. This couldn't be happening to her. *Why* was this happening to her? She'd had a hot, passionate fling with a man she'd always been attracted to. They'd used protection… She wasn't supposed to end up pregnant! This wasn't how her life was supposed to go.

And in a couple of hours, she had to go onstage, act charming and auction off the father of the baby that might be growing in her womb. *Noooo…*

Rachel pulled her up to standing position and cupped her face, her eyes radiating support and sympathy. "Alex, there's nothing you can do about it now. In the morning, we'll go and buy you a pregnancy test and I'll hold your hand while you do it. For now, try to set it aside. We have a function to host, an evening to orchestrate."

Alex heard a couple of unladylike curses leave her lips. "I won't be able to concentrate until I know, Rach."

"You won't be able to concentrate if you do," Rachel pointed out.

"No, it'll be better if I know. I far prefer to deal with reality than what-ifs." Alex sucked her bottom lip between her teeth and felt the sting of tears. "I have to know, Rach."

Rachel wrinkled her nose. "We need you here, Alex."

Alex pushed her shoulders back and blinked away her tears. "And I will be, Rachel. I promise you, I won't let you down. I'll run to the superstore just out of town and I'll use the facilities there to do the test. I'll be back in thirty minutes, forty at max."

Too many people had let her down, pregnant or not, so she wouldn't do that to her best friend. She'd made a commitment to this evening and she'd honor it, baby or not. But she had to know. It was a burning compulsion, a primal need.

Rachel shrugged. "Okay."

Alex gave her a brief hug, pulling away before she completely lost it and started to ugly cry. She handed Rachel the clipboard, and then she all but ran to the door, yanked it open and slammed into a hard wall.

Another set of hands held her biceps; this time they were far bigger and rougher than Rachel's but oh-so familiar. Alex inhaled Daniel's distinctive scent and lifted her eyes to his chiseled face, sweeping them over his sensual lips and meeting his dark, brooding eyes.

Then, to her mortification, she heard a suppressed sob escape and felt the trickle of tears down her cheeks. Daniel's grip tightened on her biceps as she rested her forehead against his chest. God, she couldn't do this, she couldn't be pregnant.

"Lex, what's wrong?" For a moment, she wished she could lay her fears on him, allow him to enfold her into his strong arms, trust him to hold her up, have her back. But that was foolishness—she couldn't trust anyone. There was only one person she could rely on and that was herself. After all, she couldn't lose herself.

"I… It's nothing for you to worry about."

He remained silent as he lifted one hand to gently stroke her hair,

And, man, even though she knew she should pull away, she couldn't bring herself to. Not yet. Just once, it would be nice not to have to stand alone and be strong, to allow someone else to carry some of her burden.

But that wasn't the way she operated.

Even so, Alex relished the feel of Daniel's hand on the back of her head, his lips against her temple. "Lex, I need to know what's upsetting you."

He almost sounded like he cared. But that was a lie. He loved her body, loved making love to her, but he didn't care enough. Not to stick by her when things got tough, when she asked him to choose her.

She'd made the mistake of relying on him when she was a teenager, and she knew not to do that again.

Alex shoved away from Daniel, swiped annoyed fingers across her eyes to wipe away the tears blurring her vision and sent him a hard smile. "I've got to go."

"Wait! What's wrong with you?" Daniel demanded. "Why are you crying? Dammit, Alexis, talk to me!"

She sent him a quick brittle smile. "Talking wasn't part of the deal when we were lovers, Daniel, even less so now. If this turns out to be something you need to know, I'll tell you, but for now, butt out! Okay?"

Alex moved away from Daniel, but she clearly heard the words he threw at her back. "You're crying, Lex! How am I supposed to let you just walk away?"

Alex turned, walked backward and spread out her hands. "It's not like it's the first time we've done this, Daniel. Ten years ago, I walked away from you in tears and you let me go. Let's repeat history, okay?"

Daniel watched Alex stride away from him, bunching his fists as he fought the urge to go after her, to shake her until she spilled her secrets. But, God, she was right. They weren't lovers anymore and even when they were—a handful of hookups over the past two months—they hadn't spent their time talking. That wasn't what they'd wanted from each other...

They'd wanted sex, hot and fast and furious. They'd wanted deep kisses and gliding hands, bone-melting pleasure and mindless nights, an escape from the day-to-day world that they lived here in Royal. They'd always, even when they were kids, had the ability to separate themselves from reality, to pretend that the outside world didn't exist. And they'd done that again, using sex as an escape, as a way to divorce themselves from their lives.

When they were entangled in one another's arms, he wasn't a Clayton and she wasn't a Slade. They were just Dan and Alex, two people who'd once loved each other with all the force and fury that was only possible when you were a teenager, before life showed you the million shades of gray between black and white. He shook his head at his youthful folly; he'd been such a sap for her.

But his days of being a sap for anyone were long over.

"Are you just going to stand there, staring into space?"

Daniel looked into the room that he'd been told was where the bachelors and Tessa were supposed to wait and saw Rachel standing by the refreshment table, her arms crossed and her eyes narrowed.

"Can you tell me what that was about?" he asked. Rachel was Alex's best friend and the two were said to be close. But how close? Like him, Alex had never been one to wear her heart on her sleeve and they rarely, if ever, had deep and meaningful conversations. Did she have those types of conversations with Rachel? Had she had them with another lover?

And why did that thought feel like the tip of a

burning cigarette incinerating his stomach? He had no claim on Alex. There was nothing between them but one blissful summer long ago and some recent hot sex.

He had no claim on her. He didn't want to have a claim on anyone and most definitely didn't want someone to have a claim on him. With attachments came pain and he was happy with his own company, to live his life alone.

People, and their expectations and emotions, drained him.

"Is there anything you can tell me?" Daniel demanded, shoving his hands into the front pocket of his battered jeans. In an hour or two he would swap his jeans and flannel shirt for a designer tuxedo, but for now he was comfortable. With what he was wearing, at least.

"Nope," Rachel replied, shaking her head. She lifted her clipboard. "I have a ton of work to do."

"And that is why I'm really surprised Alex bolted out of here like her tail was on fire. With her work ethic, normally you'd have to pry her away with a crowbar."

"I don't know what you want me to say, Daniel."

Tell me what's going on! Tell me why Alex was crying. Tell me something, anything to help me understand. Daniel rubbed his hands over his face, before turning to head out the door. He needed a whiskey, possibly two. Anything to help him numb his worry about Alex, his annoyance that he'd agreed to be part of this dumb auction. Not to mention the vague apprehension that no one would bid on him, the bastard son of Royal's wildest child.

God, now he sounded like a loser wallowing in self-pity. He'd brought The Silver C back from the brink of ruin, was regarded as one of the most talented young ranchers in the state. He was rich, respected. Who the hell cared that his mother was a crazy narcissist who was incapable of love and that his father had walked out on them before he was born?

"Daniel."

He was about to step through the door when he heard Rachel speak his name. He turned around slowly and saw the anxiety in her eyes. Oh crap, this was bad. "Yeah?"

Rachel hesitated and blew air into her cheeks. "Nothing. Ignore me."

Daniel growled his frustration and threw up his hands. "For God's sake, Rachel! What?"

Rachel's hands were white against her clipboard. "Tonight, later, when you run into her, just be gentle, okay?"

And what, in the name of all that was holy, did that mean?

Three

Daniel loved his grandmother—he did—but right now, he didn't like her. Not even one little bit. It was her fault that he was dressed in this stupid suit with a noose around his neck. She'd nagged him until he agreed to take part in this auction, and he'd finally relented, thinking that it was easier to say yes than listen to her harangue him. It was because of her that he'd have to go and stand on that stupid stage while his old ex-girlfriend and his recent ex-lover auctioned him off like a piece of meat.

And his grandmother's latest little surprise? Well, as one of the most eligible bachelors in the area, and one of the wealthiest, she'd informed him about meeting with a lifestyle reporter who was covering the auction. She and the journalist had discussed the possibility of Daniel giving an interview on whether his hopes and expectations of this evening lived up to the reality...

He had only one hope—that he managed to keep control of his seldom-seen-but-explosive temper—and exactly zero expectations.

And his grandmother was doomed to be disappointed. He had no intention of doing any damn interviews.

"Hi, Daniel."

Daniel whipped his head up and saw Tessa Noble standing by the refreshment table, her hand holding a quiche. Judging by the comments his grandmother had recently sent his way, he knew that she hoped that he and Tessa would finally connect, but unfortunately he only had eyes for an annoying blue-eyed blonde. But...*hot damn*. Tessa had always been attractive but tonight she was smokin' hot.

"Tessa? God, you look...incredible." Daniel shoved a hand in the pocket of his pants. "What are you doing here?" As soon as he asked the question, he had his answer. "Wait... Are you the surprise?"

Of course she was. It was classic Alex, when the crowd was expecting one thing, to do the exact opposite. And Tessa, looking like five million dollars, was a hell of a surprise.

"Guilty." Tessa blushed.

"Everyone will definitely be surprised," Daniel said. *Oh, smooth, Clayton. Just tell the woman that her normal look is subpar.* Which it so wasn't. "Not that you don't look good normally."

"It's okay, Daniel. I get it," she mumbled around a mouth full of quiche. "It was quite a surprise to me, too."

Distracted, Daniel leaned his shoulder into the wall, darting a quick look toward the door, hoping to see Alex. He'd sent her a couple of text messages, asking if she was okay, but she'd yet to respond. He needed to know whether, at the very least, she'd stopped crying. If she hadn't, she'd not only go on-stage with red eyes, but he might be compelled to kick someone's ass. If she ever deigned to tell him whose ass needed kicking.

Daniel turned his attention back to Tessa. "You must be tired of people telling you how different you look. How did Tripp and Ryan react?"

There was something between her and Ryan, something more than the best friends they professed to be. Any idiot could see it and maybe that was why he'd never asked Tessa out on a date. Subconsciously, he supposed he always felt that if he asked Tessa out, he would be violating the bro code. And since Ryan was a good friend, that wasn't happening.

"Neither of them has seen me yet. I'm a little nervous about their reaction."

She had a right to be. Ryan would take one look at her and, if he was as smart as Daniel knew him to be, would take her to bed and keep her there.

"Don't be. I can't imagine a man alive could find

fault with the way you look tonight." Oh crap, that had come out wrong. "Or any night…of course."

Tessa laughed and Daniel smiled at her, feeling at ease in her company.

Tessa walked toward him and laid a hand on his arm. "You know why I feel like a fish out of water. But are you okay? You look out of sorts."

He really had to try to look like he was enjoying this evening, like he was looking forward to meeting his date. He wasn't, but as a Clayton he had a duty to his community and to the event. He wanted Alex to succeed, he wanted this evening to be a resounding success. He just didn't want to stand there, wanting one woman while being auctioned off to another…

Damn you, Gran.

Normally Daniel would deflect the question, change the subject, so he was surprised to find himself giving Tessa an honest answer. He sighed heavily, the frown returning to his face. "For one thing, I'd rather not be in the lineup. I'm doing this at my grandmother's insistence."

"She seems like a perfectly reasonable woman to me." Ha! When his grandmother wanted something, she was as subtle as a combine harvester, or as an F5 tornado. "And she loves you like crazy. I'm pretty sure if you'd turned her down, she would've got over it pretty quickly."

She really didn't know Rose Clayton. His grandmother would make her displeasure known. Quietly but consistently. He shrugged, feeling the need to explain. Damn, Tessa Noble was easy to talk to. Strange that he could talk to her and not want to rip her clothes off, but with Alex, he wanted to do the exact opposite. "I owe my grandmother so much. I don't know where I would've ended up if it wasn't for her. Makes it hard to say no."

As difficult and demanding as she could be, Daniel would do whatever he could to make his grandmother happy. She'd taken a lost boy of mixed heritage and made him the man he was today. He owed her, well, a hell of a lot. Everything.

Daniel thought the subject was closed, but then Tessa spoke again. "You said 'for one thing.' What's the other reason you didn't want to do this?"

Oh damn. The last thing he wanted to do was to get all touchy-feely here. But, God's honest truth, the thought of making small talk with another woman, listening to her flirt, feigning interest in her life while the woman he really wanted to be with wanted nothing to do with him, made him want to put his fist through a door. Or a wall.

As easy to talk to as Tessa was, there were some things he'd never discuss. With anybody. He'd especially never admit to his ongoing, long-term obsession with the girl next door.

"Okay, bachelors and bachelorette."

Daniel heard Alex's command and forced himself to turn around. When he did, he noticed that not only had she entered the room but so had the rest of the bachelors who were up for auction. But his attention was completely captured by Alex. He started at her face, looking for signs of tears, and yep, her eyes were red. But her face was composed, and she had her emotions under control. Daniel released the breath he'd been holding and allowed his eyes to rove. Her hair was pinned up into a sexy knot, and her makeup was expertly yet subtly applied. His eyes widened as he took in the plunging high-slit silver dress she wore like a second skin. It was obvious that she wasn't wearing a bra and he had to wonder whether she'd forgone panties, as well.

Daniel licked his lips.

She looked magnificent, sexy, ravishing, so damn doable. He wanted to go caveman on her by tossing her over his shoulder and taking her straight to bed. Or following her down to the nearest flat surface. Hell, even a door or a wall—he wasn't picky.

Dammit. He'd seen lots of beautiful woman before, and had bedded several of them. But Alex was beyond beautiful. She was… God, what was that word? *Alluring? Captivating? Entrancing?* All three and more?

He wanted her. The thought that he always would terrified him.

"The proceedings will begin in about ten minutes, out in the gardens—which, you have to admit, look amazing. It looks like a real winter wonderland!" Alex said with a wide smile. "So, finish eating, take a quick bathroom break, whatever you need to do so you'll be ready to go on when your number is called."

Alex was in tough-girl mode, and damn, that prissy, bossy voice coming from that sexy mouth sent all his blood rushing south. Daniel resisted the impulse to bang his forehead against the nearest wall and settled for biting the inside of his lip until he tasted blood.

Act like the adult you are, Clayton.

Alex issued another set of instructions, none of which he listened to, his eyes too full of her to take in anything she was saying. How hard could it be? Walk on, try not to scowl, get sold, walk off.

At the end of her lecture, Alex smiled again, and Daniel immediately recognized that fake-as-hell, I'm-trying-to-act-normal expression. The other men in the room might have had all their brains fried by the combination of Tessa Noble looking super hot and Alex Slade looking super sexy, but in the small part of his brain that was still functional, he knew that something was up with Alex. Something life changing, crazy making, worry inducing. He could see the tension in her shoulders, the tight cords of her neck. And that blinding smile didn't come anywhere near her sky blue eyes.

Daniel started to go to her but then her gaze clashed with his and he easily read her request not to approach her, her guarded expression telling him that she couldn't deal with him. Daniel lifted one eyebrow, a silent appeal, asking her what the hell was going on, and she gave him the tiniest shake of her head.

Daniel tapped his shirt pocket, where the outline of his cell phone was clearly visible, hoping she'd understand that he needed to know, even if it was only by text message.

A tiny nod, but Daniel didn't fool himself into believing that his phone would soon buzz with an incoming message. Alex had only acknowledged his request, not agreed to do what he asked. The woman had her own mind and, God, he liked her that way.

Frankly, he liked her any damn way he could get her.

"Six thousand dollars, ladies, for Lloyd Richardson. Who has seven?"

I'm pregnant.

Alex acknowledged a bid from Gail, Tessa's friend, and that bid was quickly topped by Steena Goodman. Alex briefly wondered what these women saw in Lloyd to make them go that high. Gail, looking sulky but determined to have her date with Lloyd, raised her paddle again. Well, she'd have to pony up because Steena had deep pockets and her wealthy now-dead husband's money to spend.

She was pregnant with Daniel's baby.

It was like two halves of her brain were operating independently. One half was playing the role of the merry, if slightly manic, auctioneer, while in the other half, she was curled up in a fetal position, battling for breath.

Grandpa's first great-grandchild is going to carry Clayton blood.

"Eight thousand dollars, Gail? Wow, that's super generous." *Too generous*, Alex thought, alarm bells ringing in her head. Gail didn't look like she had that sort of money lying around. "Oh, a new bidder at nine thousand dollars! Marvelous."

She had to tell Daniel…and Gus. Daniel would have to tell Rose and, God, what fun that was going to be.

"Fifty thousand dollars."

Alex blinked at Steena's outrageous offer. She couldn't possibly have heard her right. Alex looked at Rachel, who was standing to her right, and judging by Rachel's shocked expression, she knew that her hearing wasn't faulty. Steena Goodman had just bid fifty thousand dollars for a date with Lloyd. Was she out of her ever-lovin' mind?

But knowing her money was good—those weren't fake diamonds hanging from her ears and decorating her fingers—Alex gripped the gavel, preparing to sell Lloyd to the woman before she came to her senses. She flashed a smile at Rachel and lifted her gavel.

"One hundred thousand dollars."

Oh no. Oh hell. Oh crap. Alex widened her eyes at Gail's ridiculous offer, waiting for her to wave the offer away, to tell her it was a joke. But Gail just kept her eyes on Lloyd, one hand on her hip. A low buzz swept through the room as the drama unfolded. Alex knew that she should sell the date, that nobody—not even Steena—would top Gail's ludicrous bid. She also knew that there was no way that the charity would see a hundred thousand dollars from Gail.

Call it a hunch.

Alex looked toward James Harris, the new TCC president, and he lifted his hands in a what-can-you-do gesture. Maybe she was judging a book by its cover; maybe Gail did have a hundred grand to spare. This was, after all, Texas, where anyone could be a billionaire. It had happened before.

Alex dropped the gavel, hiding her trepidation. "Lloyd Richardson has been sold to Gail Walker."

Gail clapped her hands like a little girl getting an award and skipped up to the stage to fling her arms around Lloyd's neck. He responded by laying a hot kiss on her. Gail kicked up her foot and Alex immediately noticed the scuff mark on the back of the heel of her shoe. Oh boy, this wasn't going to end well.

Alex felt a little dizzy as she watched Lloyd and Gail leave the stage. She was exhausted and overwhelmed. Two more to go and then she could go home and collapse.

Tessa wouldn't be a problem; she'd just have to watch the bids roll in. But Daniel? Well, hell, crap and damn. How was she going to sell her baby's father to another woman?

Alex, after spending thirty excruciating minutes accepting congratulations on the success of the evening, slipped out of the festively decorated gardens and headed toward the TCC clubhouse.

She needed some time alone to get her racing heart under control, to reflect on this crazy day, to think, dammit!

Wrapping her arms around her waist, she stepped inside the clubhouse and headed for the small office James had allocated for auction-related business. After closing the door behind her, she flipped on a desk lamp and half sat, half leaned on the wide wooden desk.

Selling a date with Tessa had been a dream, as she'd barely been able to keep up with the flurry of bids for her gorgeous friend. Tessa had looked surprised at the attention she garnered and then relieved when Ryan topped all the other bids with a whopper offer. She'd caught Tessa's pleading look and quickly closed the bidding, accepting Ryan's overly generous bid with a quick snap of her gravel. Maybe there had been a man in the audience who could top Ryan's bid, but Tessa had been a good sport and she deserved a date with Ryan. And maybe, finally, the two of them would figure out what the rest of the community already knew: that they should only date each other. Permanently.

Selling a date with Daniel hadn't been as easy. Rachel, bless her, had offered to take over as auctioneer but that would've caused speculation they could ill afford. So she'd gritted her teeth, pasted on a bright smile and, after fifteen excruciating minutes, she sold Daniel to an oil baron's daughter from Houston: a tall, cool brunette with a predatory look in her eyes.

She'd wish him luck—everyone knew Iona Duckworth had a thing for cowboys. And cowboys who also owned and operated one of the most iconic ranches in the state? Jackpot!

Alex dropped her head, finally able to devote her full attention to the problem at hand. She was pregnant.

With Daniel's baby.

God.

Alex stared down at the exotic wooden floor. How did this happen? Why was life punishing her like this? She wasn't ready to be someone's mom, and couldn't imagine being fully responsible for another life. Moreover, she knew nothing about babies—except how they were made, and apparently she didn't know enough about that! How on earth was she going to raise a child, accept Mike's amazing offer to be a partner in his new start-up and… God!

Through this child growing inside her, she was now connected to Daniel forever. Well, at least until their child became an adult, but that was long enough. Once she told Daniel about the baby, he'd be a permanent and constant part of her life, exactly what she'd been trying to avoid when she told him that they had to stop sleeping together. She didn't want Daniel in her life—she couldn't cope with all the emotions he pulled to the surface, all the memories, the resurgence of the hopes and dreams she'd had as a stupid-with-love teenager.

Being close to Daniel, even if it was just a physical thing, was dangerous enough. But this child, their baby, would require them to find a way to interact, emotionally. Emotional interaction led to attachments and she didn't do attachment.

Though, apparently and according to the three pregnancy tests she'd done earlier, she had no choice but to become attached. That was what happened with moms and babies, wasn't it?

Oh God, she was going to be a mommy.

Alex heard the door to the office open and then she felt Daniel's arms around her. Her bones liquefied, and she fell into him, utterly exhausted and emotionally winded. She didn't think she could take much more tonight.

"Lex. God, honey, what the hell is going on with you?" Daniel demanded, lifting her up and pulling her into his body.

Should she tell him now or later? What was the point of delaying? This news wouldn't be any easier to hear tomorrow or a month from now.

Daniel held her head with one hand and for a moment she felt safe, not so very alone. If she told him now, he'd push her away from him and she'd lose this closeness, this support. Should she tell him? How could she not?

"Lex, you're scaring me," Daniel said with concern in his voice. "You're as white as a sheet and you're trembling. I'm starting to freak out here."

He was freaking out? And he hadn't even heard the life-altering news yet.

Alex wound her arms around his waist and rested her forehead on his chest. Once she told him, she'd have to build another wall between them, reinforce her barriers. It would be so easy to allow Daniel to take control—he was a take-charge and do-what-I-say type of guy. He was an alpha male, supremely comfortable with making quick decisions, plotting a course and following it.

And she was so tired, feeling so utterly over-whelmed that it was tempting to let him take control, to follow his lead. But at some point, she'd start to rebel and argue. Or worse, she might—although, given her contrary nature, this wasn't likely—start to like him taking charge. No, she was the captain of her own ship.

Even if her ship was currently a leaky rowboat with a broken oar.

Alex gathered her courage and stepped out of Daniel's arms. Pushing her hair off her face, she met those deep, dark worried eyes.

"Dan, I have something to tell you. You're not going to like it."

He lifted one eyebrow. "What can be worse than having to spend *any* time with the cowboy-obsessed Iona Duckworth?"

Oh, she could easily top that. "I have a date for you that's going to last the rest of your life."

Surprise and shock skittered across Daniel's face. Then panic set in. He lifted up his hands and took a step back. "Lex, it was just an affair. We haven't spent enough time together to make those sorts of pronouncements. You don't know me anymore."

If her heart wasn't threatening to jump out of her chest, she might've laughed at his erroneous assumption. "I'm not talking about you and me, Daniel!"

Relief replaced panic and Alex ignored the flare of disappointment. He'd once spent hours with her, painting their future, but now the thought was abhorrent. Yes, they'd grown up, they were adults now, and she'd packed up dreams of her and Daniel a long time ago.

It shouldn't hurt but it did. Far too much.

This, *this*, was why she had to keep her emotional distance, why she had to spend as little time with Daniel as possible. With him, foolish thoughts, remembered dreams and unwelcome emotions crept in and threatened her unattached heart. She'd planned on walking away from him and Royal—leaving all these pesky emotions behind. But if she left now, she'd be taking a part of Daniel with her...

"Seriously, I'm about to shake your news out of you," Daniel muttered.

"I'm pregnant, Daniel."

His guttural bark was short on amusement and long on disbelief. "That's not funny, Alex."

"I know. It really isn't. And I really am pregnant."

Alex walked around her desk, pulled her bag out from the bottom drawer and shoved her hand inside. She pulled out the three pregnancy tests and threw them across the desk. Daniel picked up each one in turn, saw the positive indications and Alex watched a muscle jump in his tight jaw. His sensual mouth was now a slash in his face and his olive skin turned pasty. The news was finally starting to sink in…

"It's mine?"

What the hell? How dare he ask that? She dramatically slapped her hand against her forehead. "Oh, wait, *no*! It could be one of the many other men I was sleeping with at the same time I was sneaking around with you!"

Daniel shoved his hand through his hair, pushing an errant curl off his forehead. He sent her a sour look. "Still as sarcastic as ever."

"It's my default response to stupid comments," Alex shot back. She walked out from behind her desk, sat on the corner and crossed her legs. "I'm newly pregnant, just a few weeks."

Daniel released a couple of f-bombs and followed those with a string of creative curses. When he was done, he stopped pacing, stood in front of her and curled his big hands around her bare upper arms. The heat of his hands burned into her skin as lust burned through her. Her desire for him surprised her; she'd thought that the news of her pregnancy would've killed any thoughts of sex.

But no. She wanted him as much as ever.

"What do you want to do, Alex?"

She lifted one shoulder. "What can I do? It's here."

"You're not considering an—getting rid of it?" Daniel asked, obviously worried.

"You wouldn't want that?"

He shook his head and she noticed his bleak eyes, the desperation. "This sucks. It's not what either of us wanted, but…it's a consequence of the choice we made. We have to deal."

We. Not *you.* On hearing that one small word, Alex relaxed a fraction. She wasn't in this alone… not entirely.

Daniel rested his forehead against hers, released another swear word and sighed. "I'm sorry, Alex. Jesus, this wasn't supposed to happen."

Alex heard the buzz of her phone and looked down at the desk. She frowned at the message that popped up on her screen. It was an SOS from James Harris, of all people. The auction was done and some of the guests had already drifted away. What on earth could've happened that warranted three SOS texts and a terse "We have a major situation"?

She also noticed two missed calls from James and four from Rachel.

"I need to go."

"Uh, *no.* We need to discuss this, Alex!"

"Something has happened—"

"Damn right something's happened. You're pregnant with my child. I want to discuss this, find a way forward."

Yep, alpha male. Alex remembered her grandmother's words, heard Sarah's voice in her head.

Start as you mean to go on, honey. And don't take any horse crap.

Alex pulled away from his strong grip. "The baby will still be here tomorrow, Daniel, and the next day. We have time." She could see that her answer irritated him, but she didn't much care. Daniel liked having all his ducks in a row, knowing where they were going and how to get there. He'd once confided in her—a moment that was both random and rare—that living with his mom was like standing in a bucket on a raging river, not sure when or how he'd be tossed into the rapids or over the waterfall. He liked planning his own route, being in control of his destination.

She understood that, and they would sit down and have a decent conversation, but right now the bachelor auction had hit a snag and she was needed.

Daniel threw up his hands. "I cannot believe you are walking out on me. You've just told me that we are having a baby, Alex!"

Alex drilled her index finger into his chest. "*I* am having a baby, Clayton, not *we*. Do not think that you can stomp into my life with your size thirteens and take over. That's not going to happen." She huffed out a breath. "When I am ready to deal with you, with the situation, I will give you a call."

Daniel's eyes widened at her strong statement. Good. The sooner he realized she wasn't a pushover, the better off they'd both be. *This is what happens when you spend your time together making love and not talking*, Alex realized. Assumptions were made.

And babies, too.

She picked up her cell phone, walked toward the door and slipped into the hallway. Pushing away thoughts of that big gorgeous, confused man she'd left behind inside, she walked down the hallway to James's office.

Another fire to extinguish. Hopefully this would be the smallest, as well as the last, of the evening.

Four

In the parking lot of the TCC, Daniel glanced at his watch and grimaced. It was after 1:00 a.m., and he was exhausted. Tired and worried and, yeah, completely freaked out.

He was going to be a dad. Holy crap. He'd never had a father, or even a proper male role model, and as a result he knew next to nothing about being a good father. He was going to be responsible for a tiny human life…a terrifying prospect for someone who didn't have the smallest idea about what to do or how to be a dad. Fatherhood, a state he'd thought he'd only consider far into the future, was a nebulous concept, something as inexplicable as black holes or the binary code.

There was nothing Daniel hated more than the fear of the unknown.

Thanks to his erratic and unsettling childhood, he found security in planning his life, breaking down his future into five-, ten-, fifteen-, twenty-year goals. But to be honest, those plans were all ranch and business related, he hadn't spent a lot of time planning his personal life.

Or any at all.

Leaning back against Alex's sports car, he linked his hands behind his neck and stared up at the vast Texas sky. All his energy—every drop of sweat and blood—went into making The Silver C Ranch the best it could be. He knew and loved every inch of his land and he knew that the ranch was his place, his corner on earth. People came and went, but his grandmother and The Silver C kept him stable as a child and anchored as an adult.

According to Alex's earth-tilting news, the first of the next generation of Claytons was baking inside of her, and what did that mean? For Rose and for the future of The Silver C? And what did it, *should it*, mean to him?

Having children wasn't something he'd thought much about, and when he did, it was only in terms of who would inherit the ranch sometime in the very distant future. Honestly, at this point in his life, he didn't want to be a dad and he had no interest in being tied down—he was perfectly content with brief affairs and one-night stands, keeping emotionally distant. But Alex… Dammit. Well, she'd recently managed to narrow that distance, to pull him closer. She tempted him to unbend a little and to open up a fraction, probably because he subconsciously wanted a way to recapture some of the magic and joy of that heady summer so long ago.

It had been the happiest three months of his life, so why wouldn't he want to experience it again? But she'd been right to call it off, to make them move on. What he hadn't expected was that they'd be left with a lifetime memento of their fling.

They'd made a child. God. He was utterly determined to be a better parent, and the exact opposite of his mother—and to be a stable, responsible and hands-on dad.

His child would know that he loved him, or her, that he would be a constant and consistent part of his child's life. That was nonnegotiable. His child would know his, or her, father's love. *His* love…

He wanted to be there for the big and small things, and that meant having his baby's mother in his life. But Alex… Being with Alex made him feel alive, uncontrolled, impulsive. The way she made him feel terrified him. But he'd just have to deal, find a way to keep her at arm's length, because he planned on being a vital part of his child's upbringing. He wanted to change diapers, do the midnight feedings, pace the floors while he tried to put his child to sleep. He'd do whatever was needed, but in order to be a part of his child's life, he had to be *in* that life. That meant marriage—*God!*—or at the very least, him and Alex living together.

Where could they live? Since Alex lived in the main house at the Lone Wolf Ranch, his house was the most reasonable option. Or they could build a new place, something that suited them both. And they'd have to tell their grandparents—that was going to be a barrel of laughs…

First things first, Clayton. Talk to Alex, offer to marry her, secure his child's future. As for the way Alex made him feel, well, he'd simply have to get over that. He would not allow her to cause him to lose control or focus. They could marry and within that union they'd be friends, even lovers, but he'd always keep himself emotionally detached. It was safer that way.

Daniel heard footsteps and lifted his head to see Alex walking toward her car and him. Cold air caught in his throat as the rest of his body heated, then sizzled. Man, she looked amazing, so damn sexy. When she noticed him leaning against her car, she released a long sigh. She was past exhausted, he realized, and a wave of protectiveness swept over him. He was right to feel protective over her, he rationalized, because she was the mother of his child. By protecting her, he protected his son. Or daughter.

When Alex reached him, he lifted his hand and ran his knuckles over her pale cheek. "You look done in, honey," he said, his voice gruff.

"It's been a hell of a night," Alex replied, surpris-

ing him by resting her butt on the side of her car.
She'd pulled a jacket over that sexy dress, but her
shapely thigh slid out from under the high slit in the
skirt. He wanted to pull the slippery material up and
find out for sure whether she was wearing panties
or not.

Like that was important! Daniel mentally slapped
himself as he moved to stand in front of her. They
had a future to discuss, plans to make.

Alex held up a hand and he saw that her eyes were
red-rimmed and that she now sported blue stripes
under her eyes that her makeup could no longer con-
ceal. "Not tonight, Daniel. I can't take anymore."

He curbed his impulse to push and tipped his head
to the side. "What was the great bachelor-auction
emergency?"

"Ah, that. Well, that hundred-thousand-dollar bid
Gail made for Lloyd was a fake bid—neither have
that type of money. To distract a reporter from report-
ing on that juicy piece of gossip and totally ruining
the success of the evening, we've offered the reporter
complete access to Ryan and Tessa's super romantic date. And to distract him further—" Alex's eyes
narrowed in the moonlight "—you are, according to
Rose, giving an interview to the same reporter on
what it feels like to auction yourself off and how it
feels to be one of Texas's most eligible bachelors."

Daniel waited for Alex to laugh, to give him any
indication that she was joking, but she just sent him
a steady look with no hint of amusement. So, ah,

this interview was going to happen whether he was on board or not.

Crap.

Daniel closed his eyes and gripped the bridge of his nose. "My damn interfering grandmother."

"Tonight, I am grateful for her interference. The two stories will be a welcome distraction from the fake bid."

"I swear, my grandmother only hears what she wants to! I'm going to kill her. I swear I am!"

"She'll just come back and haunt you," Alex said behind a yawn. "Look, Mr. Most Eligible, I am exhausted, as it's been a hell of a day. I'm going home."

But they hadn't talked about the baby or come up with any concrete solutions. Daniel started to argue but then he saw the sheen of tears in her eyes, noticed that her hands were trembling. *Stop being an ass and think about her for one sec, Clayton. She's been on her feet for fourteen hours, she's just found out she's pregnant and, after hearing that news, she still managed to stand in front of a huge crowd and pull off a super successful event.* Alex had grit and courage in spades—he had to give her that.

Making a quick decision, he took her bag off her shoulder and shoved his hand inside, looking for her car keys. Ignoring her protest, he wound his arm around her waist and lifted her up to walk her around the car, pulling open the passenger door.

"What the hell are you doing?" she demanded as he bundled her into the seat.

"Taking you home."

"I can drive," Alex protested.

Daniel crouched down between the car door and its frame and placed his hand on her slim thigh. "Lex, let me do this for you. You are played out and I don't want you making the drive back to the Lone Wolf exhausted and emotional."

Alex licked her lips and sighed. "I was going to go to the tree house, spend the night there. I need some space, to be alone."

"I'll take you anywhere you want to go, honey. I just want to make sure you get there in one piece," Daniel said, keeping his tone noncombative.

"What about your car?"

Daniel shrugged. "It'll be safe enough here." He moved his thumb to stroke her bare thigh. "Let me take you home, Lex."

Alex dropped her head back against the headrest and gave a quick nod. Daniel gathered the rest of her dress, put it inside the car and slammed her door shut. In the five minutes he took to adjust her seat to his longer legs, back out of her space and reach the TCC gates, she was sound asleep.

"No, I'm not going to marry you, and I'm not going to move in with you, either."

With her battered cowboy boots propped onto the railing of Sarah's tree house, Alex held Daniel's hot stare and shook her head to emphasize her point. However, Daniel, dressed in faded, formfitting denims and a green-and-black flannel shirt worn over a black T-shirt, tried to scowl her into submission. But she'd been raised by Gus and had learned at an early age to stand her ground or get run over.

When he started to argue his point—again!—Alex rushed in, "Daniel, we are not living in the 1800s. My honor, your honor, is not at stake. Sure, Rose and my grandpa are probably going to blow a gasket, but they will just have to deal. I am not jumping into a marriage with you or into sharing a house just because I'm pregnant. That's a terrible reason to be together!"

"I want to see my child, Alex." Daniel pushed the words out from between clenched teeth.

"He or she will arrive in only seven months' time. How will us moving in together or getting married help you with that right now?"

Daniel opened his mouth to issue what she knew would be a hot retort only to have the words die on his tongue. Ha! He didn't have an answer to that argument! And there wasn't a reasonable answer because he was being an idiot!

She dropped her feet to the ground and rested her forearms on her thighs. "Daniel, I have no intention of denying you access to our child, but this idea you have of you being a full-time dad—that's not going to happen." Alex caught the flash of pain in his eyes, knew that her words were harsh but it was better to clear this up now before expectations were created that could not be fulfilled.

She was not eighteen anymore and dreaming of this man, fat babies, horses and a life on the ranch, filled with laughter and love. Dreams were for children, for the naive, and she far preferred cold reality. "We're not going to be a couple and we are not going to live together. I've had a business offer. I'm probably going to take it. It's lucrative and it's in my, and the baby's, best interest for me to accept it since my bills are going to quadruple."

Daniel's eyes turned cold. Oh damn. Now she'd properly insulted him.

"I am fully capable and prepared to pay for everything you or the baby need."

Of course he was, the guy was a millionaire fifty times over. That wasn't the point! "And I am an independent, successful woman who can earn her own money and support her own child," Alex stated, her voice dropping ten degrees. Standing up so that she did not feel like Daniel was looming over her, she slapped her hands onto her hips and handed him her most ferocious scowl. He didn't look remotely intimidated, dammit.

"I do not need you, or any other man, to pay my way."

"Goddammit, woman, you are so contrary!"

"Pot. Kettle. Black." Alex threw his words back in his face.

Daniel threw his hands up in the air, whipped around as if to leave and, before she could blink, he'd spun back and he was in her space, his fingers tunneling through her hair and his mouth falling toward hers. Alex knew that she should stop him but instead of pushing him away, she stood on her toes so that she could feel his lips against hers a second sooner. Waiting even a moment longer than she needed to was torture. She wanted him, of course she did, always had. Probably always would.

He drove her nuts. Nobody had the power to annoy her as intensely as Daniel could but, God, when he kissed her, he morphed from Irritant Number One to Sex God to Have-to-Get-Him-Naked-Immediately.

Those amazing lips moved over hers and his hand on her butt pulled her into him. Denim rubbed against denim and underneath the fabric she could feel the evidence of his desire. They might not know how to be friends and had even less idea of how to co-parent. But, God, this? This they knew how to do.

Daniel's tongue slid into her mouth to tangle with hers, and she groaned deep in her throat. She should stop this; it wasn't sensible. This would just further complicate a crazy situation, but instead of pushing him away, her hand skated up under his T-shirt to find hot, hard skin. Daniel had the same idea, since his hand was down the back of her loose jeans, cupping her bare backside with his big calloused hand.

He yanked his mouth off hers to speak. "I've got to know, were you wearing panties last night? Under that sexy dress?"

It took Alex a moment to make sense of his words. She'd worn the tiniest thong she had and really, she still didn't know why she bothered. But she wasn't about to admit that to Daniel. He wanted to hear that she'd worn nothing more than that silver slip dress. "No."

Alex felt him tighten and harden, saw the fire in his eyes and knew that there was no going back. They were headed for the bedroom, or the sitting room. Hell, they might not even make it inside.

Daniel pulled her long-sleeve T-shirt up and over her head, looking down at the sheer lacy bra she wore. She was in the early stage of her pregnancy, and she'd yet to feel different, but Daniel was looking at her like she was made of spun glass, of delicate platinum strands. His index finger gently traced the outline of her nipple and she sucked in her breath, watching his dark hand against her lighter skin. Even in winter he looked tanned, courtesy of his Hispanic heritage. So sexy, Alex thought as he pushed the lace away to touch her, skin on skin. Daniel bent his knees, wrapped his big, powerful arms around her thighs and lifted her so that her nipple was in line with his mouth. Holding her easily, muscles bunching but not straining, he tongued her, pulling her nipple into his mouth, nibbling her with his teeth. She ran her fingers through the loose curls he hated, tracing the shell of his ear, the strong cords of his neck.

"I want you, Lex. I know I shouldn't but, God, I do," Daniel muttered, pulling away from her to look up, his eyes blazing with lust.

"Dan…"

He rested his forehead between her breasts, still holding her, and she felt his ragged breath against her skin. She knew that he expected her to ask him to let her go, to step away, but she couldn't. She didn't know how to be a mommy, to have Daniel in her life, how to navigate her suddenly complicated future, but she knew how to make love to this sexy, infuriating man.

She loved being naked with him.

"Take me inside, Dan. Love me until I can't think anymore," Alex whispered, brushing her fingers across his lips, his jaw.

Daniel flashed her a grin that was sexy enough to melt glass, and then he carried her inside. Allowing her to slide down his body so that their mouths could meet, he kissed her as he navigated his way to the bedroom at the back of the tree house. With long hot slides of his tongue, and hands possessively skimming her skin, he silently demanded that she match his passion. Alex held on to him as he lowered her to the bed and sighed when he settled into the V shape between her legs. Right place, far too many clothes.

Her shirt was gone, so Alex pulled his over his head and tossed it to the floor. She sighed when his naked chest touched hers and lifted her head so that she could tongue his flat, masculine nipple. A good start but not enough.

"Please, Dan, I don't want to wait. It's been too long."

Daniel heard her pleas and pulled back to yank

her boots off her feet and tug her jeans down over her hips. His eyes moved down, stopping on her breasts before moving over her still-flat stomach to her relatively modest bikini panties.

His eyes widened and he released a low chuckle. God, he had a great smile. It crinkled his eyes, revealed his straight white teeth and hinted at the tiniest dimple in his right cheek. But as much as she liked seeing his smile, she couldn't understand why he was laughing.

Alex pushed herself up to rest her weight on her bent elbows.

Daniel arched an eyebrow. "I'm game if you are."

Ah...what was he talking about? They'd had great sex but nothing weird or kinky, so where was he going with this?

Daniel gestured to her panties and Alex tried to read the slogan upside down. Okay, but Afterward We Get Pizza?

She groaned. She was *not* wearing her sexiest lingerie. "They were a gag gift from Rachel," she explained, blushing. "I haven't had a chance to do laundry."

"Silk or cotton, I can pretty much guarantee that anything you wear will always end up on the floor."

Daniel slowly peeled the panties down her legs, his smile still tugging at the edges of his gorgeous mouth. He dropped the panties to the floor and stood up to undress. Lifting his feet, he pulled his boots off, then pushed his jeans over his hips, taking his underwear with him. Embarrassment forgotten, Alex stared at him and Daniel stood there, allowing her to look her fill. Broad shoulders, muscled arms, that wide chest. He had sexy abs, but she also adored those long hip muscles, his lean, powerful thighs, the arch of his surprisingly elegant feet.

Daniel was a curious combination of masculine grace and rugged good looks, but beneath it all, he was a man of honor. By marrying her, he wanted to do what was right, what he thought was best for their baby. She respected that, respected *him*. But she couldn't marry him or move in with him; she shouldn't even be making love to him.

But this…thing…between them ran too deep and she couldn't resist him. She would always, as long as she breathed, want him but she wouldn't let herself love him. She couldn't afford to do that, to let him hurt her again.

Daniel placed his hands on the bed on either side of her face and placed his mouth on hers, sipping, tasting, exploring. They'd had slow sex, hot sex and crazy sex up against a door, but his kisses seemed different tonight, intense with a hint of gentleness. Alex slipped her tongue into his mouth and tried to dial up the passion. Hot and fast she could deal with, but she didn't know how to handle slow and sexy and profound.

She lifted her hips to make contact with his shaft, wanting to get out of her head and fully into the physicality of the act. Daniel didn't take the hint so she ran her thumb up his dick and when she stroked his tip, he jerked and then groaned.

"Need you, Dan, now." And she did. She needed him to remind her that this was all sex, that she couldn't have the ranch and the horses and the hot baby daddy in her life. Dreams like those put her heart at risk...so she'd just take the sex.

It was simpler that way.

Daniel nudged her legs farther apart with his knee before stroking her secret folds with his fingers. "You're so wet, Lex."

"Because I need you, Dan. I need sex." Alex heard the desperation in her voice and didn't know whether she was trying to convince herself or him.

He pushed inside her and Alex wrapped her legs around his back, pulling him closer. Heat, warmth, completion. The rest of her life was crazy confusion but, as Daniel started to move, Alex realized that this made sense. It was the only thing that did.

As he pushed her higher and higher, the needs of her body stilled her whirling thoughts and all she wanted was more of him. Her hands skated over his back, his butt, down the backs of his thighs. A strand of hair landed in her mouth and she thrashed her head from side to side as he kissed her neck, pulled her earlobe between her teeth. She was so close, teetering on the edge of pleasure, when she heard Daniel's demand to let go, his reassurance that he would catch her.

She wanted to stay here, just for another minute, bathed in that silver light of anticipation. "Dammit, Lex, I can't hold on," Daniel muttered.

Placing his hand between their bodies, he found her clit and stroked it, just once with his thumb. It was the sexual equivalent of a hard hand shoving her between her shoulders and she plunged over the cliff... Falling, falling, shattering. But he fell with her, his body shaking as he came.

Daniel collapsed on her and Alex didn't mind that her breath was shallow, that his body weight pushed her into the soft mattress. When they were lying like this, intimately connected, they were at peace. It was only when they started to talk that things went wrong.

Alex pushed her nose into his neck, kissed his skin and ran her hand down his spine. Beautiful but stubborn. Gorgeous but flawed.

Just as she was, contrary and imperfect.

Daniel pulled himself up and gazed down at her, holding his body weight on one hand as he pulled the strand of hair from her mouth and tucked it behind her ear. Alex saw her confusion reflected in his eyes. Then determination replaced confusion and she knew that he was looking for the right words to use to convince her to come around to his way of thinking.

Okay, she might be stubborn but he was relentless.

"I'm not marrying or moving in with you, Clayton. No matter how good you are in the sack."

"Dammit." Daniel slipped out of her, stood up and stalked to the small bathroom attached to the bedroom. "You are a stubborn pain in the ass!"

Sure she was but that didn't make her wrong!

Five

The end of January

Gus heard the door to his study open and looked up to see his still-beautiful Rose, and his heart, old and jaded, thumped against his rib cage. He'd waited for fifty-plus years to see that soft smile on her face, for her to walk into the room and into his arms.

Man, he was riding the gravy train with biscuit wheels.

Rose placed her hands on his chest and her mouth drifted across his.

"Mornin', husband."

He was her husband. And how freakin' great was

that? He smiled, allowed his hand to drift down over her ass and grinned. "Mornin', *wife*."

After a little canoodling—the best way to start a morning—Rose rested her head on her chest and sighed. "Have you had any more thoughts on what to do about our grandchildren?"

During their wedding reception last night, Rose dropped the bombshell news that Alex was pregnant and that Daniel was the baby's father. Strangely, instead of feeling angry, he'd felt content. Like this news was right, simply meant to be. He'd initially thought that he was so very relaxed because he'd been floating on a cloud of wedding-induced happiness, but upon waking this morning, it still felt right, like it was preordained.

He wasn't, however, happy that Alex and Daniel were going to try to raise their great-grandchild separately and not as husband and wife. That wasn't acceptable. Not because he cared about convention or how it would look, but because, dammit, those two were meant to be together.

They'd meant to be together ten years ago—shame on him and Rose for making their grandchildren casualties in their stupid, long-held feud—and they were meant to be together now.

"My Alex is 'more stubborn-hard than hammered iron.'"

Rose pulled back and smiled her appreciation. "Shakespeare, Gus Slade? I'm impressed."

Gus felt his ears heat at her admiration and then

shrugged it off. They had more important things to worry about. "So, about these darned kids…"

He refused to allow them to repeat his and Rose's foolishness and waste so much time. They had to re-unite Alex and Daniel and, after showing his wife exactly how much he loved and wanted her, he'd spent a good part of the night working out how to do just that. "I have a plan, but it might involve a sacrifice on our part."

"Okay. How big a sacrifice?"

Oh man, she wasn't going to like this. "Our honeymoon. I'm sorry, sweetheart. I want to spend some time with you alone and I know you want that, too—"

Rose stepped away from him, pulled a chair from the dining table, sat down and crossed her legs. She didn't look mad but, since they'd been married for less than a minute, what did he know? "Gus Slade, I have waited fifty-two years to be your wife and I don't care about going away for our honeymoon." A soft radiant smile lit up her lovely face. How could she possibly be more beautiful today than she was half a century ago? Yet she was. "Being with you—whether it's here in Royal or at Galloway Cove or on the damned moon—is where I want to be."

"Such language, darlin'." Gus tsk-tsked.

Rose rolled her eyes. "I'm not a fragile flower, Gus. Neither am I sixteen anymore. And I can swear if I *damn* well want to."

Gus hid his smile with his hand. But before he could investigate this saucy new side of his wife—

man, that word just slayed him, every single time—
he saw the speculation in her eyes.

"Tell me what you have in mind, and I'll gladly
sacrifice our week on Matt's island to get those two
to see daylight."

Gus outlined his plan and watched as Rose stared
out the window at the east paddock, where his old
paint horse, Jezebel, was keeping company with his
prized Arabians and Daisy, the airheaded goat.

"Do you think it can work?" Rose asked him, worry
in her eyes. She no longer wore her mask of aloofness
and he was clearly able to read her concern for both
Daniel and Alex. He could see her deep desire to see
them happy. Rose didn't wear her heart on her sleeve,
but that didn't mean she didn't feel things deeply,
sometimes too deeply.

Gus sighed. They'd wasted so much time being
angry with each other, but he couldn't regret loving
Sarah—they'd had a good marriage. Losing his son
so early had been horrible but raising his grandkids
had given both him and Sarah a second lease on life.

Rose's life hadn't been so easy. Her daddy had
been a hard man and Ed, her husband, had been as
cuddly as a hornet and had made her life hell. They'd
made so many mistakes, but he was damned if he'd
watch Alex and Daniel repeat their history. They
might argue like crazy but the room crackled with
electricity when the two of them were together. They
owed it to themselves and their baby to make it work.

"Gus? Will your plan work?"

He shrugged and, needing to touch her, held the back of her neck. "I hope so, honey."

Rose nodded and leaned her head against his side. "If it doesn't, we'll lock them in the barn until they come to their senses."

Gus laughed, thinking she was joking. When she remained silent, he looked down at her. "You're joking, right?"

Rose stood up and wound her arms around his waist. "We're giving them the chance to come to their senses in a nice way. After all, it's the least we can do after everything we pulled to keep them apart. But if it doesn't work, we'll do it the hard way." He saw her stubborn expression and grinned. His wife was fierce. And he loved her that way.

He loved her, period. Always had.

The first week of February

Alex sat on the leather seat of the private plane Gus hired to fly his bride to Galloway Cove for their honeymoon and wished that she could ask the pilot to close the doors and whisk her away to Matt's stunning private Caribbean island. She couldn't think of anything she'd rather do more than stretch out on white sand beneath a blue sky, read a book and just be.

But no, before he left, her grandfather wanted to give her one last lecture and that was the only reason why he would've asked her to meet him and Rose on the plane. He'd leave her with a reprimand about doing the right thing, raising her baby with its father and not as a single mom in Houston.

She was depriving Daniel of being a full-time dad, depriving Gus and Rose of having quick and easy access to the baby, making life ten times harder for herself without having the support of Daniel, as well as her family and friends.

Yada yada.

She knew that—how could she not? Being on her own in Houston, trying to run a company as a single mom, was going to be the hardest challenge of her life! But Gus didn't understand—she doubted anyone would—that was less scary than remaining in Royal, utterly in lust and half in love with her baby's father. The best chance she had to stop thinking about Daniel Clayton and the life she could never have was for her to move back to Houston. She had a far better chance of pushing him out of her mind there than here in Royal.

If she stayed here, she might just do something crazy.

"Grandpa, Daniel and I had our chance."

"That doesn't mean that you can't have a second one," Gus replied.

It was like talking to a brick wall. In an effort to get through to him, Alex pulled out the big guns. "One of the reasons we missed our chance was because you and your new bride were vehemently opposed to us being together."

Gus hesitated before replying. "We might not have been completely correct in that assumption."

Okay, that was as close to an apology as she was going to get from her taciturn grandfather.

"But in our defense, you were also very young."

"Daniel," Alex reminded him, "chose The Silver C over me. His loyalty to Rose and to the ranch has always been stronger than any love he had for me."

She hadn't been able to explain further, unable to admit to Gus that she couldn't trust that Daniel would be there for her and her baby when life got tough, couldn't tolerate the thought of being second or third on his list of priorities.

"I think you are making a mistake, Alexis," Gus quietly told her.

"But, Grandpa, it's my life and my mistake to make," Alex insisted.

"Except it's not—you have a baby to think of," Gus replied before ending the call.

Why couldn't he understand that she'd lost so much? If she and Daniel lived together, raised their child together, there was a good chance that she would fall in love with him again; of that she had no doubt. Wasn't that the reason she'd broken up with him recently, because she could feel herself sliding downhill into love?

Alex had lost Daniel's love once, and she'd mourned him for years. Their breakup had been another type of death, and she was done with death, of all types.

She wouldn't survive another loss. Her shattered heart would crumble into pieces too fine to be patched back together again. And while she had no intention of denying him access to his child, she needed to start getting used to being on her own, to a life that didn't have Daniel in it. He was her baby's father, not her lover and definitely not her friend.

It was better, safer, this way. Gus might've found love after a half century—and she was truly happy for him—but his path wasn't hers. She didn't want love in her life, it hurt too damn much when it left.

If only she could get Gus, and by extension Rose, to understand that.

Alex heard footsteps and turned to look down the aisle, expecting to see the happy couple. Oh crap. Daniel. Maybe she wasn't in for a lecture; maybe Gus and Rose simply wanted a glass of champagne with their two favorite people before jetting off for a week of sun and sand and sex—*ooh, can't go there*. Sun and sand was descriptive enough.

Daniel took the seat opposite her and looked at the open bottle of champagne sitting in an ice bucket. "We're here for a dressing-down, aren't we? This time they are going to tackle us together?"

Alex wanted to think otherwise but she nodded. "Probably."

Daniel placed his boot on his ankle and Alex noticed that his denims, soft from washing, had a rip at the left knee and that the hems were frayed. She pulled in a deep breath and her womb throbbed at the intoxicating scent of soap, sun and ranch life mixed with pure, primal alpha male. She'd missed him so much. Keeping her distance was torture but so very necessary.

"Thanks for answering my fifty million calls," Daniel bit out, pulling his designer shades off his face and hooking them onto the neck band of his T-shirt.

"Don't exaggerate," Alex retorted.

"Stop evading the subject. You've been avoiding me for weeks and I don't like it." She had. Leaving Royal for Houston for a couple of weeks helped. She'd needed to meet with Mike, discuss their partnership agreement and get a feel for his business, but the fact that she was half a state away from Daniel had helped with her evasion tactics.

"I saw you at the wedding," Alex pointed out.

"Where you refused to discuss anything to do with the future and the baby. We have plans to make, Alex! We need to know where we are going!"

"Do we really have to go through all this again?" Alex threw up her hands and leaned forward. "I am going back to Houston. I am taking a partnership in a start-up company, and you are staying here. In five months I will give birth."

"What about visitation rights? A nanny to help you? Child support?" Daniel bellowed.

"We can sort that out later when—" Alex broke off when she noticed the attendant approaching them. The young woman stopped, stood in the aisle alongside them and tossed them an easy smile.

"Sorry to interrupt but we've just had word that Mr. and Mrs. Slade are running a little late. But we need to move the plane so that the next aircraft can take our slot."

Alex looked at Daniel and they both shrugged. "Okay?"

That bright, mischievous smile flashed again and Alex saw that her name tag read Michelle. "Safety regulations state that we can't taxi without you both wearing a seat belt. Regulations, you know?"

"For God's sake!" Daniel muttered, reaching for his seat belt and pulling it over his waist. "Do you have an idea when they might be here? I need to get back to the ranch. I have a meeting in an hour." He frowned at Michelle, as if it were her fault their grandparents were late.

Michelle watched Alex buckle up before turning her attention back to Daniel. "They should be here soon, Mr. Clayton."

Alex felt the aircraft move forward as the pilot guided the plane to its new position. The attendant walked away and Alex reached for the bottle of champagne and a crystal glass. Now, this was the way to fly. And if Gus had meant this champagne to be for Rose, then he should've been prompt. Besides, any sane woman needed alcohol while dealing with Daniel Clayton. It was deeply unfair that that much sexy covered a whole bunch of annoying.

Before she could tip the bottle to her glass, the champagne was whisked from her hand and the bottle dropped back into the ice bucket. "Not happening."

Alex glared at Daniel. "When did they make you the no-champagne-for-breakfast police? Last time I checked, I'm an adult and I can have—"

"Cut it out, Alex. I'm the dad who's telling his baby's mom that she can't have alcohol while she's pregnant."

Alex wanted to lash out at him, tell him that he had no right to tell her what to do, but dammit, on this point he was right. She couldn't drink alcohol while she was pregnant. Gah! What had she been *thinking*? Probably that she needed the soothing power of the fermented grape, especially if she had to deal with Mr. Impossible.

Alex risked looking at Daniel and saw the smug smile of his face at winning that minor battle. Annoyed, she kicked out and smiled when the toe of her right boot connected with his shin.

"Ow, dammit!" Daniel howled before bending down to rub his injury.

"Don't be a baby, Clayton." Alex looked out the window, saw that the plane was whizzing past the trees bordering the airport and frowned. "Aren't we going a bit fast?"

"Don't kick me again," Daniel warned and followed her gaze to the window. He released a low curse. "We're not taxiing."

Alex gripped the arms of her seat. "Daniel, what's going on?"

"If I'm not mistaken, we're about to take off." Daniel looked around, saw an electronic panel and jabbed at the button labeled Attendant.

"This is Michelle. What can I do for you, Mr. Clayton? Miss Slade?" Michelle's melodious voice drifted over them.

Daniel didn't waste time looking for explanations. "Stop this plane right now or I'm going to have you all arrested for kidnapping." Alex shivered at the I'm-going-to-kill-someone note in his voice. She'd only heard that voice once, maybe twice, before and she knew that you didn't disobey Daniel Clayton when he used it.

"Sorry, sir, but we can't do that. Besides, Mr. and Mrs. Slade promised to pay all our legal fees if you decide to sue us. Plus a hefty retainer."

"What the hell are you talking about?" Daniel asked, his eyes widening.

Alex immediately understood why. They'd left the ground and they were literally jetting off to God knew where.

"There is an iPad in the side pocket of your seat," the airline attendant continued, and Daniel kept his eyes locked onto Alex's face as he dropped his hand to the side of his seat.

"Switch it on and there's a video clip on the home screen. It should answer all of your questions," Michelle stated, and Alex heard the click as she disconnected the intercom.

Daniel booted up the iPad, glared down at the screen and impatiently jabbed the screen. He leaned forward so that she could see the screen and there, looking far too pleased with themselves, were their respective grandparents.

"Yes, we've kidnapped you. Yes, we are bad people," Gus said, sounding utterly unrepentant.

Rose jabbed him with his elbow and stared into the camera. "Alexis and Daniel, we are sorry for being so intransigent a decade ago. We should not have pulled you into our little dustup and we apologize."

Only in Texas could people call a fifty-year feud a dustup.

Gus leaned forward, his blue eyes serious. "That being said, it must be noted that you two are the most stubborn creatures imaginable and unable to see what's in front of your faces. To help you with your lack of vision, we are sending you to Galloway Cove in our place. Matt's house is the only one on the island, and it is fully stocked with everything you might need. We packed a suitcase for each of you, which Michelle will give to you when you land."

Daniel hit the pause button, looked at Alex and shook his head. "I'm adding breaking and entering to the charges I'm laying against her."

Alex rolled her eyes and tapped the play button so that the video could continue. Gus picked up the conversational train wreck. "The plane will return in a week and, by then, we want a proper, thought-out, reasonable plan on how you two intend to raise this child together. And by together we mean in the same house, preferably the same bedroom."

"Just to be clear, marriage is our first choice," Rose added.

"When hell freezes over," Alex muttered. On-screen, Rose smiled, oblivious to their anger. Which was exactly why they recorded this message and didn't video call them. Alex snorted. Cowards.

"And don't try to bribe the pilot and his crew to turn around. We already told them we'd double whatever you offer." Rose, looking pretty and content, blew them a kiss. "One day you'll thank us for this!"

"Not damn likely," Daniel muttered.

The video faded to black and Daniel tossed the iPad onto the seat next to him. He groaned and covered his eyes with his hand. Alex opened her mouth to speak but no words emerged. She tried again—nothing—and shook her head. Had Rose and Gus lost it completely? "They can't do this," she whispered.

"They just did," Daniel shot back, pulling his phone out from his back pocket. He hit a button, dialed a number and waited impatiently for it to ring. "Voice mail."

"Gran, I am not happy! What the hell gives you the right to meddle in our lives? We're adults and your actions are reprehensible and unacceptable. Have you completely lost your mind?"

Knowing that Gus rarely carried his phone and that when he did he was prone to ignoring it, Alex called her younger brother, Jason. He answered on a rolling laugh.

"Not funny, Jason! I'm on a plane because Grandpa has arranged for us to be kidnapped. Tell him to turn this plane around. Better yet, just let me talk to him."

"He's not here, sis. Or if he is, he's keeping a very low profile, if you get my drift. He is, after all, on his honeymoon."

Ew. The words *Gus* and *honeymoon* did not sit well next to each other. "I don't care what you have to do but find him and tell him to turn this damned plane around!"

Another chuckle. God, when she saw Jace, she was going to throttle him. "Grandpa told me to tell you, if you made contact, to pull on your big-girl panties and suck it up."

"*Find. Him.* Tell him that this isn't funny, that we want to come home!"

"Are you mad? You've been sent off to stay in a luxurious house on a private island in the Caribbean. It's windy, wet and cold here in Texas, and our grandfather is getting more action than I am. My heart bleeds for you! As I said, big-girl panties—"

Screw big-girl panties, she was going to take off her thong and strangle him with it! "Find Grandpa," she muttered, death in her voice. "Tell him what I said."

Alex disconnected the call and rubbed her forehead with her fingertips. "It looks like we're going
to Matt's island."

"Looks like?" Daniel snapped back, his expression blank but his body radiating tension.

Alex sent a wistful look at the champagne bottle.
"Don't you think this warrants a little champagne?
For medicinal use only?"

"No, you're pregnant. No alcohol."

Daniel narrowed his eyes at her, pushed the intercom and ordered a whiskey, straight up. He looked at
Alex and his small smile was just shy of evil. "But,
as you said, this situation warrants alcohol."

Alex responded to his smirk with one of her own
and deliberately, swiftly kicked him again.

After playing Daniel's voice message to Gus, Rose
lifted her eyes to meet his. His body, like hers, was
older and they didn't have the energy they once had.
But his eyes were still those of a young man's, with
the power to stop her in her tracks. And underneath
the layer of mischief, she saw his grit and determination, his rock-steady calm. Gus did what he needed
to do and always stayed the course.

"He is not a happy camper," Gus commented.

"I've seen him lose his temper and it's not pretty,"
Rose admitted, pushing her phone away. She picked
up her coffee and took a sip.

Gus was silent for a good twenty seconds. "Would
he hurt her?"

"Hurt Alex?" Rose demanded, horrified. "Good God, no!" When Gus still looked skeptical, she placed her hand on his arm. "No, honey, he would never hurt her. He witnessed his mom being slapped around, beaten up, and he'd never hurt a woman or a child."

Gus's eyes softened with sympathy. "His rough childhood must have done a number on him."

Rose nodded, not bothering to hide her sadness from her man. They were married, so she could share anything, and everything, with him. "Stephanie... God, Gus, she was so wild. I couldn't tell her a damn thing—never could. She hit thirteen and entered self-destruct mode."

"I don't know whether she's alive or dead. When she lost custody of Daniel, she refused to have any contact with us."

"And that happened when he was twelve?"

Rose released a quavering breath. "He spent the summer of that year with me, and when Stephanie came to fetch him, he told her that he wasn't going back with her. Neither would he let me pay her to let him stay."

Rose knew that her chin was wobbling. "He told her that he was staying with me, that he was going to go to school in Royal. That if she made trouble for him or me, he'd go to the police and detail every drug deal he saw, finger every dealer she had, tell the police about every 'uncle' who lifted a hand to him." She released another breath. "She had a choice—she could leave him with me without a fuss or he'd make life very, very difficult for her. Stephanie chose to leave him with me."

"And he never spoke to her again after that?"

Rose shook her head. "Neither of us have."

She ran her finger around the rim of her cup. "I can't help thinking that if I'd done some of this and not that, loved her more, disciplined her more, gave her more time and energy, she would've turned out better."

"Sometimes there is no better, Rosie."

"She's her daddy's daughter—she's Ed through and through. Mean, aggressive, malicious." She saw the concern on his face and quickly shook her head. "Daniel isn't like that. He's a good man, Gus. You'll see that eventually."

Her husband pondered her words. "The TCC members seem to think so. The younger members trust him implicitly and they say he has integrity." Gus smiled at her. "I'm looking forward to knowing him, darlin'. It's time to put the past to bed, and young Daniel has done nothing to me."

"Except get your granddaughter pregnant," Rose replied.

Gus shrugged. "The way those two look and act around each other, I'm just grateful it didn't happen when they were teenagers."

"He's the best thing—apart from you, recently— that's ever happened to me. I can't lose him, Gus."

Gus took her hands is his and waited until her

eyes met his. Then he squeezed her hands. "You're not going to lose him, Rosie. I promise you that."

"He's so mad…"

Gus shrugged. "Let him be mad—he'll get over it. In a little less than an hour, he'll be on a deserted island with a beautiful girl he's crazy about. Trust me, he'll be thanking you soon."

"I doubt it," Rose retorted. "They just might kill each other. Or maybe they'll wait to do that until after they've killed us." She frowned at him. "Why are you looking so chipper? Didn't you get a nasty voice mail?"

Gus's cocky smile belonged to the young man she knew so long ago. "Prob'ly did. Don't carry my phone. No doubt that Alex has sent Jason an annoyed message to give to me."

Rose shook her head in exasperation. "You've got to start carrying a phone, Gus. What if I need to get a hold of you?"

"Not a factor." Gus lifted her knuckles to kiss her fingertips. "I don't plan on being a couple of feet from you anytime soon." His mouth curved as she moved her hand to his cheek. "But I am thinking of getting another phone, one that only you have the number to."

"That would make me feel so much better," Rose told him. "I don't want to be that woman who constantly keeps track of her man, but you know…in case of an emergency."

Gus's smile turned wicked. "To hell with an emergency. I'm only getting it in the hope that you'll call me up for a—what do the kids call it—booty call?"

Rose's shocked laughter bounced off the walls. "Augustus Slade!"

Gus looked at her, his face full of love. Then he waggled his eyebrows to make her laugh. "Anytime you have the urge, I'm your guy."

He really was her guy. And damn if she didn't have one of those urges now. Rose looked out the window and saw that it was ten o'clock on a cold, wet winter morning in February, not the time a woman of a certain age should be slinking upstairs. But to hell with that; this was supposed to be her honeymoon. Rose took his hand, grinned and stood up.

"Come upstairs and rock my world, handsome."

It was Gus's turn to look utterly poleaxed, but that didn't stop him from leaping to his feet with all the energy of a twenty-year-old.

Six

Upon landing at Galloway Cove, Michelle lowered the steps to the private jet, stowed their suitcases in the back of the golf cart parked to the side of the landing strip and tossed them a jovial smile. "Have fun." With that, she ran back up the steps to the plane. Minutes later the jet was in the air and headed back to Houston.

Alex climbed into the golf cart and sat down next to Daniel, her thigh brushing his. Leaning forward, he pulled off his flannel shirt and threw it into the back of the cart, before placing his hand on the wheel and cranking the small engine.

Tired of their silence, Alex darted him a look. "Any idea where we are?"

"West of the Bahamas."

Alex wrinkled her nose at his brief reply. "Can you tell me anything about where we are going, what to expect?"

"Matt is one of the wealthiest guys in Texas. All I know is that the house is completely secluded, has its own private beach and reef. It will be jaw-droppingly amazing." He gritted his teeth. "The other thing I know is that I need to get the hell off this island. I've got a ranch to run. I can't just take off on a Monday morning with no warning!"

"You've said that before, numerous times," Alex told him testily. "Look, you might as well accept that we are stranded here until that plane returns." She gestured to the awesome view of a flat turquoise-colored sea. Below them, nestled against the cliff and partially covered by the natural vegetation, they could see the tiled roof of what she assumed to be Matt's beach house. She gestured to the well-used track in front of them. "The sun is shining. The sea looks amazing. So, on the bright side—"

"There *is* no bright side," Daniel muttered, and Alex gripped the frame of the cart as he acccler-ated forward.

"I can't think of anything better than lying on the beach for a week. I'm exhausted and it will give me time to think. We don't even have to talk to each other. Actually, it would be better if we didn't."

Clenching his jaw, Daniel steered the car along the track, and Alex heard the cry of a seagull and the sound of a rushing creek above the cart's rumble. Daniel kept moving his head from the path to look at her and back again. Annoyed, she half turned in her seat and glared at him. "What? Why do you keep looking at me like that?"

"What about sex?"

"Where did that out-of-left-field question come from?" Alex lifted her hands in confusion.

Daniel's dry look suggested she get with the program. "We're together. Alone. On an island. We might be as frustrated as hell with each other and the situation, but you cannot be that naive to think that, with our sexual chemistry, we're not going to end up in bed."

She wanted to deny his words, but she knew she would come across as being disingenuous if she brushed off his comment. Alex lifted her thigh up onto the bench seat, her knee brushing his hard thigh. After marshaling her thoughts, she picked out her words. "Daniel, we've known each other for a long time but we don't *know* each other."

"What do you mean?"

She'd been thinking about this a lot lately. She and Daniel communicated with their bodies, not with their minds. They were both guarded people and they both struggled to let people in. They knew each other's bodies intimately, knew exactly how to behave naked. But fully clothed? They were like drunken cowboys stumbling around in the dark. As her baby's father, Daniel was going to be in her life for a long time, so didn't she owe it to herself and their child to get to know his mind a fraction as well as she knew his body?

"Let's be honest here, we've always been sexually attracted to one another, and even as teenagers, we far preferred to make out than to talk—"

"And it's still my first choice."

Although tempted, Alex ignored his interruption. "That trend continued when we hooked up. I don't know you—not really—and you certainly don't know me."

Daniel sent her an exasperated look. "Of course I do."

Alex snorted. "Rubbish. Let's test that theory, shall we?"

Daniel released a frustrated sigh. "If you're going to ask me a dumb-ass question like what is your favorite color, then I won't know."

Alex thought for a minute. "No, let me start with an easy one. Do I prefer to shower in the morning or at night?"

Daniel hesitated before guessing. "At night."

It was a good guess. "What do I like on my pizza?"

He hesitated and she pounced. "You don't know. Neither do you know whether I have allergies and I don't know if you vote."

"Of course I vote!" Daniel retorted.

Alex ignored him. "Do you believe in God? What are you currently reading? What is your favorite sea-son? Are you on social media? What is your favorite meal? Who is your closest friend?"

"Yes, sort of. A Corben novel. Fall. Hell, no, I don't have time to post crap no one cares about on Facebook. Beef stew. And yes, I have friends... Matt. Ryan. I talk to James Harris pretty often, too."

She'd said *closest* friend, not friends in general, but she'd still found out more about him in thirty seconds than she had in ten years. How much more would she find out about him if they actually conversed instead of kissed?

"We're going to be raising a kid together, separately but together. Should we not use this time to get to know each other better?"

Daniel steered the cart around a corner and Alex was momentarily distracted by the magnificent house in front of them. It hugged the side of a cliff, and trees and natural vegetation cradled the house like a mother holding her child. A massive wooden door broke up the sprawling white expanse and Daniel parked the cart to the right of it. Leaving the cart, she turned to take her bag but noticed that Daniel already had it in his grasp, as well as his own duffel bag.

She smiled her thanks and watched as he walked up to the front door. Alex took a moment to appreciate his long-legged, easy grace, the way his big biceps strained the bands of his T-shirt, the width of his shoulders. It was brutally unfair that he was the walking definition of sex on feet. Alex sighed and watched as Daniel placed his hand on the door. It swung open from a central pivot and he stepped back to motion her inside.

Alex stood in the doorway, unwilling to go inside until she had an answer from Daniel. "So, are we going to try and get to know each other a little better?"

"We can try," Daniel replied. He shrugged and looked down at her with those deep, compelling eyes. "But I guarantee you that, thanks to the combination of sand, sea and you in a tiny bikini, you're going to be under me sooner rather than later."

Arrogant jerk, Alex thought, walking into the beach house. How dare he think that he could just click his fingers and she would lie down, roll over and let him scratch her tummy. Sure their attraction was explosive, but she wasn't so weak that she'd just fall into bed with him—

Oh my God, this place is fantastic.

Alex stopped in her tracks as she drank in their luxurious surroundings. It was open plan, as all beach houses should be, with high vaulted ceilings displaying intricate beams. As soon as they stepped out of the hall and into the living space, the eye was pulled toward the massive floor-to-ceiling windows, across the infinity pool to the view beyond. Alex was momentarily unsure where the pool ended and the sea began. Stepping forward, she spared a glance at the sleek kitchen, the wooden dining table and the chairs that were the same blue as the sea. Under comfortable sofas, an expensive rug covered the floors, but it was the view that captured her attention: it was the only piece of art the room needed. The white beaches, the aqua sea, the lush emerald of an island in the distance.

"Holy crap."

Alex turned to look at Daniel but he was equally entranced by the house and the view. Dropping their bags to the floor, he strode over to the windows and looked at the frame. Within seconds, the windows turned into sliding doors, and warm, fragrant air rushed into the room. Alex walked out onto the covered deck and looked left and then right. "It looks like the deck runs the length of the house. I imagine all the bedrooms open up onto it. We can sleep with the doors open and listen to the sound of the sea."

Daniel looked down at the tranquil sea and lifted an eyebrow. "It's as calm as a lake—I doubt we're going to hear the sound of crashing waves."

"Don't be pedantic—" Alex's eyes widened when she saw Daniel bend over to pull off his boot. When his feet were bare, he pulled off his T-shirt before attacking his belt buckle and ripping open his fly. "What the hell are you doing?" she demanded.

He gave her a wicked smile and gestured to the pool. "Going for a swim."

His hands slipped under the fabric of his jeans and Alex squeaked when she saw that he was stripping them off. "You're swimming naked?"

Daniel shrugged as his clothes pooled at his feet. "We're totally alone and you've seen it all before."

She had and every inch of him was absolutely glorious. "You're not going to help our cause of not sleeping together if you're going to parade around buck naked, Clayton."

Daniel's smile broadened. "That's your cause, Slade, not mine. I intend to get to know you and sleep with you. I also plan to spend a great deal of time trying to convince you not to go to Houston. If you won't marry or move in with me, then I want you as close as I can possibly have you."

"I—you—argh!" Alex, annoyed by his cocky smile and his self-assurance, threw up her hands. She did, however, watch that magnificent body dive into the pool.

After his swim, Daniel pulled on his wet clothes and padded barefoot into the house. Not seeing Alex in the living area, he picked up his bag and walked down the hall, opening doors as he went along. Study-cum-library, gym—nice—and a sauna. He entered the first bedroom he came to and threw his bag onto the massive double bed, taking a minute to appreciate the view. Like he suspected, the floor-to-ceiling windows were in fact another set of doors, and he immediately opened them, welcoming fresh air into the room. This room was super nice but he wouldn't bother to unpack; he would end up sharing whatever bedroom Alex chose.

Which, if he knew her, would definitely be the master suite.

Daniel pulled his phone out of his pocket and checked for a signal, of which there was none. Cursing, he tossed it onto the bed and left the room to head for the study. If he was going to stay on this godforsaken island, he would have to send some emails, leaving instructions for his foreman, his PA and his business manager. And he would drop his grandmother another message, reminding her how out of line she was.

Daniel sat behind Matt's desk, pulled out the first drawer, and yep, as he thought, inside the drawer rested a state-of-the-art laptop. If Matt had a laptop, then he'd have an internet connection, which was exactly what he needed. Daniel leaned back in his chair as he waited for the laptop to boot, thinking that he could, with a couple of keystrokes, have another plane on the runway in a couple of hours.

He could hire a private plane as easily as Gus had, and this farce could come to a quick end. Except that maybe he didn't want it to…

Daniel stared out at the tranquil ocean. He was here, Alex was here and they were nowhere near Royal. They could escape their grandparents' machinations, the Royal gossips, the crazy normal that was their day-to-day lives. They could both take this week to find a way forward, to have some heart-to-heart conversations, to plot a course.

He still wanted to marry Alex—that was the plan that still made the most sense to him. The Clayton-Slade feud had been buried with Gus and Rose's marriage—something that Royal was still talking about—and after their nuptials, his and Alex's nuptials would barely raise a brow or two. He wanted to raise his child in a conventional family, one with a father and mother close at hand. He'd spent the first twelve years of his life with an unstable mother, constantly wishing he had a father he could run to, live with, a bigger, stronger man he could look to for protection and comfort. He never ever wanted his child to think—not for a second—that he wasn't there for him, that he was anything but a shout away. He wanted to teach his son to ride, shoot, fish. Hell, if he had a bunch of daughters, he'd teach them the same thing. He wanted them to have the run of the farm. And if his kids were Alex's, then they'd have the Slade ranch as an additional playground. He wanted them outside, on horses and bikes, in the stables, swimming in the river or in the pond. He wanted his kids to have the early childhood he never had, with two involved, loving parents.

For the sake of their kids, he and Alex could make a marriage work. They were super compatible together sexually, and they could, if he took her suggestion to learn more about each other, become friends. Friends who had hot sex—wasn't that a good marriage right there? Love? No. Love—having it, losing it, using it as a carrot or a club—just complicated the hell out of everything.

Marriage was a rational, sensible decision. He just had to convince Alex that this was the best option available to them both. Hell, even if she balked at getting married—and he had no doubt that she would—she could still move into his place. Gus and Rose wouldn't be happy at their nontraditional living arrangements, but it was better than nothing.

Right, he had a plan. He liked having a plan; it made him feel in control.

Alex leaned back against a sun-warmed rock and watched the sky change. Blue morphed into a deep purple, and then an invisible brush painted the sky with streaks of pink and orange. This Caribbean sunset was possibly one of the prettiest she'd ever witnessed, and she couldn't help but sigh her appreciation.

Alex felt warm, strong fingers graze her shoulder and she turned to look up at Dan, who held out a bottle of water. She smiled her thanks, shifted up a bit, and when he sat down next to her, she noticed the bottle of beer in his hand. He'd changed into a pair of swimming shorts and wore a pale yellow T-shirt. She wore a sleeveless tank over her bikini and her hair was a tangled mass of still-damp curls.

"Thanks."

Daniel's bare shoulder nudged hers and Alex ignored the flash of desire that ricocheted down her spine. Taking a sip from the bottle he'd thoughtfully opened for her, she gestured to the sunset. "I wondered if you were watching the sunset."

"It's stunning," Daniel murmured.

She hadn't seen him since before lunch and she wondered what he'd been up to. "So, what have you been doing?"

Daniel took a moment to answer her. "Hanging out, chilling. Seeing if I could find signal for my phone."

"Did you find one?"

"Nope."

She also had no cell phone signal, and it was a problem. She needed to talk to Mike, ask him for some more time to think about his offer, to work out the logistics of moving to Houston. "I need to send my grandpa an irate email, telling him how much I resent his interference and machinations. He doesn't carry a phone but he does read his emails."

Daniel's chest lifted as he pulled in some air. "You can."

"I can what?" Alex asked, digging her toes into the sand.

"Send an email," Daniel admitted. "I found a computer in Matt's study. I should've realized that the guy, with all his business interests, would have to have some contact with the outside world. On further examination, there's also a satellite phone for emergencies."

Alex flew to her feet. "Why didn't you tell me sooner? Why are we here? Why aren't we at the airfield, waiting for a plane?"

She could go home, confront Gus, talk to her clients, Mike. She could put some distance between her and Daniel, start her life without him. At the thought, her heart stuttered, then stumbled. She had to; she had no choice. She and Daniel didn't have a future, not as anything more than co-parents.

She wasn't marrying him or moving in with him; both options were impossible.

Daniel pulled his legs up and rested his forearms on his knees as he squinted up at her. "You're missing the sunset, Lex."

"We can go home, Daniel! We need to go home."

He gently took her wrist and pulled her back down so that she sat with her back to the sunset. The pink-and-yellow light danced across his face. Daniel's thumb stroked the sensitive flesh on the inside of her wrist.

"Let's not, Lex."

"Let's not what?"

"Go home," Daniel said, and she sent him a shocked look. He'd been furious about leaving, about being manipulated into taking this time away and now he wanted to stay?

"I don't understand," Alex said, pulling her hand out of his grasp. She couldn't talk to him and touch him—she wasn't that strong.

"As loath as I am to give those two meddlers any credit, I think that they are right. We need to work some stuff out, and we can do it here," Daniel suggested. "You're exhausted. Organizing the auction was hard work, and I haven't taken a break for nearly a year. We both can do with some downtime. And while we relax, maybe we can plot a way forward."

"You and your plans, Daniel!" Alex muttered. "You can't plan for every eventuality. Some things you have to allow to evolve, to work themselves out."

"Work themselves out? God!" Daniel released a harsh laugh. "That's such a stupid thing to say. Things very rarely work out, Alexis!"

Wow, that was quite the reaction to an innocent comment. Instead of jumping on him, Alex tipped her head to the side and waited for him to speak.

Daniel picked up a handful of sand, clenched his fist and allowed the particles to slide down the tunnel his hand created. She'd never seen such sad eyes, she decided. Sad and angry and distraught.

"Do you know what it's like to live a life lurching from crisis to crisis? Do you know how unsettling it is not to know where you are going to be, what bed you're going to be sleeping in? Whether your mother will be there when you wake up? It sucks, Alex!"

She stared at him, shocked at his outburst but even more surprised that he'd revealed that much about his childhood to her. When they were younger, she'd pried, tried to get him to open up about his life with the infamous Stephanie, but he'd never so much as mentioned his mother and what his life was like before he came to live at The Silver C. From the pain she saw in his eyes, Alex knew that it was way worse than she'd ever imagined.

"I'm sorry—"

Daniel immediately cut her off. "Forget it. Ignore what I said. My point is that I like to plan. I always will."

Because it made him feel secure, like he was in control. Alex understood that now. She picked up a handful of fine sand and allowed it to trickle through her fingers. Knowing that Daniel had said everything he intended to for now, she contemplated whether to stay on the island or to leave. She could call for a plane and within hours they'd be winging their way back to Royal and nothing, not one damn thing, would be settled between them.

But on the other hand... With a couple of emails, she could clear her schedule, take this time they both desperately needed. Didn't she owe it to herself, to Daniel and her child, to stop, to breathe? To think?

To plan? Dammit.

Alex made herself meet his eyes and reluctantly nodded. "Okay, we can stay here."

His eyes turned smoky and Alex immediately recognized that look. She held up her hand. "Hold on, cowboy. If we do this, then there are going to be some ground rules."

Daniel released a low curse, and a frown pulled those black brows together. It wasn't a surprise to see that Clayton didn't like anyone else calling the shots. Tough—it was something he was going to have to deal with. She wasn't eighteen anymore and so desperately eager to please.

"I'll only do this if we can start fresh."

"What the hell does that mean?" Daniel demanded, grumpy again.

"I am not hopping back into bed with you." Alex drew a heart in the sand and quickly erased it, hoping he hadn't noticed. "As I said, I want us to do something different, be different!"

"Lex…" Daniel muttered.

"Dan, we're having a baby together! We're not going to get married, or even live together, but if we are going to be in each other's lives, see each other every weekend, then there has got be something more between us than some hot sex."

"I'm not good at talking, Lex."

Neither was she. But they had to make an effort. "I know, Dan, and neither am I. We're not good at opening up, at sharing, but, God, the next eighteen years are going to be sheer misery if we don't start to communicate."

Daniel stared past her shoulder and Alex picked up the tension in his body, saw his hard jaw, his thin lips. She needed this, she suddenly realized. She needed to dig beneath the surface to find out what made this amazing man tick, and not only for her baby. She needed to know him. Because even if they couldn't be lovers, they could be friends, and being friends with Dan was infinitely better than being lovers and casual acquaintances. He had fabulous mattress skills but between that gruff exterior was, she suspected, a lonely guy who needed a friend. And to be honest, so did she.

Daniel's cheeks puffed and then he expelled the breath he'd been holding. When he turned to look at her, his expression turned rueful. "I can't promise you anything, but I can try, Lex. That's all I can give you."

"I still want to sleep with you, though," Dan added, being brutally honest.

"I know." Alex picked up her water bottle from the sand and dusted it off. "But we can either have one or the other, not both."

"I vote for sex."

She rolled her eyes. "You're a guy—I wouldn't expect anything else. But no, that's not going to happen. I think we need to be friends."

"Not half as much fun," Daniel grumbled.

Alex smiled at his sulky face. "Man up, Clayton."

Although his expression remained sober, she caught the amusement in his eyes. He leaned toward her, his amazing eyes on her mouth and his mouth hovered over hers. She should pull back—she *would* pull back…but how much could one little kiss hurt?

Alex frowned when she saw his lips twitch and then he resumed his position against the rock.

Oh, that was just mean.

"Jerk."

That twitch widened into a sexy, full smile. "You're easily distracted, Lex. I like it."

She nailed him with a don't-push-it glare.

Daniel's expression turned serious. "You've changed. You're not half as biddable as you used to be."

"Yeah, I grew up." Alex half turned, put her hands behind her and leaned back, stretching out her legs. She looked at the sunset—the light was slowly fading and the colors were deepening in intensity. She turned her head to look up at the house and noticed that it was fully lit. There were also lights along the entire length of the path running from the beach to the house. It looked like a totally different structure, mysterious and sexy.

Just like the man lounging next to her.

Daniel followed her eyes and whistled in appreciation. "Wow. Matt Galloway is one lucky bastard to own this place." He turned his head to look at her. "So, did you choose a room?"

"Yeah, I couldn't resist the master bedroom. When the doors are open, it's like you are sleeping outside, and it has this amazing shower enclosure. It's three walls of glass and utterly breathtaking."

Daniel's mouth twitched with amusement. "That would give anyone on the beach an eyeful."

"I thought the same thing," Alex said with a smile. "But when I walked down to the beach, I checked. It's made of that fancy glass where you can see out but not in."

Standing up, Daniel held out his hand. Alex put her hand in his and he hauled her to her feet. "I'm starving. Let's go see what's in the fridge. I think I saw some no-alcohol beers if you're interested."

"I'd far prefer a glass of wine," Alex said as she headed to the path with Daniel behind her.

"Well, I'd prefer to be sharing your bed. But apparently we can't always have what we want."

Seven

The next day, Daniel looked up and saw Alex standing in the doorway of the study. He leaned back in his chair and indulged himself by giving her a top-to-toe look. A red-and-white blousy shirt was tied at her still-slim waist and flirted with the band of the sexiest, most flattering pair of cutoff jeans he'd ever seen. Her feet were bare, as was her face, and she'd pulled her thick blond mane into a loose bundle on top of her head. She'd never looked more beautiful, and he desperately wanted to take her to bed.

Friends. They were trying to be friends.

Worst idea ever.

Daniel glanced at his watch and then grinned. It was past nine and that meant that she'd had a solid night's sleep. Good. She'd needed it. He was happy to see that the blue smudges were gone from beneath her eyes.

"Hey, sleepyhead. I'm not going to ask you if you slept well, because you obviously did."

Alex walked into the room and hopped up onto the corner of the desk, facing him. "I did. And for your information, I did wake up during the night and I did hear the sea. The tide must've been in."

Alex liked being right and he couldn't blame her because he liked it, too. He smelled the mint on her breath and forced himself not to lean forward and have a taste. Man, this week was going to be a drag if he couldn't touch or taste her.

Daniel leaned back and linked his hands across his stomach. If he kept them there, maybe he wouldn't give in to the urge to scoop her up, haul her outside and lower her to the sun bed on the porch. Excitement pooled in his groin at the thought of stripping her down until only the sun, his fingers and his mouth were touching her soft, fragrant skin...

Pull your head out of the bedroom, Clayton.

"How are you feeling?" he asked. He darted a look at the small strip of bare flesh he could see above the band of her jeans. Nobody would ever suspect that she was pregnant.

"Fine, actually. I haven't had any morning sickness or cravings for weird food." She smiled as she answered him, banging the heel of her foot against the leg of the desk. "And... Yay... I still fit into all my clothes, which is a definite plus."

Alex picked up a glass paperweight from the desk, turned it over and lifted her eyebrows. She carefully replaced it and when she looked at him again, her eyes were bright with astonishment. "That's Baccarat crystal and super expensive."

Daniel didn't care if it was a solid-gold nugget. He wanted to talk about her and the baby growing inside her. "Have you seen a doctor?"

Alex nodded. "I visited the clinic and had a blood test to confirm I was pregnant. I was prescribed some vitamins, given a handful of pamphlets to read through and was recommended a couple of books. I need to visit an ob-gyn when I get back and have an ultrasound scan. That way the doctor will get a better idea of my due date. It's also to check that the baby is growing as it should."

Daniel leaned forward, opened his online calendar and sent her an expectant look. "When is the appointment?"

"Do you want to come with me?"

She sounded surprised. "When are you going to realize that you're not alone, Lex? That we are in this together?"

Alex rattled off the date and time and Daniel tapped the it into his calendar. He was determined to be the exact opposite of his father—and his mother—who'd missed every milestone of his life, from his birth to football games to graduation.

Alex sent him a grateful look. "Thanks. Knowing you will be there will make me feel less—" she hesitated before completing her sentence "—alone. I've never missed my mom more than I have in the past few weeks and I dare not even think about Sarah. If I do, I won't stop crying."

Daniel placed his hand on her knee, his skin several shades darker than hers. He started to stroke back and forth, and then reminded himself that he was touching her in comfort, not for pleasure. "Your mom and dad died when you were pretty young. Do you remember them?"

Alex wrinkled her nose. "A little. But I'm not sure if my memories are my own or because I heard so many stories about them. I can't tell what's real or what's been planted."

"Does it matter, if they are good memories?" He didn't have any good memories of his mom, of his early life. He'd been so damn busy trying to survive, to get through the day, the week, until he could next visit The Silver C and his grandmother. On the ranch, under that big blue Texas sky, riding and exploring, he could let go, find a little peace.

Alex touched her stomach with her fingertips. "I just wish she was here."

Daniel squeezed her knee, choosing to express his sympathy through touch rather than words. Then he removed his hand because there was only so much temptation he could take.

"Have you eaten? There's a fruit salad in the fridge. Or I can make you pancakes. And bacon."

Alex's eyes widened in disbelief. "You cook?"

"Yes, smarty-pants, I can cook. In fact, I intend to catch and then cook our lunch."

Alex gestured to the ocean beyond the open windows. "I'm impressed. Maybe you should get to it, because the fish might not be in a cooperative mood. I haven't seen any fishing rods lying around."

"They are in the storage shed, along with fins, goggles and a Jet Ski. And a spear gun, which I'm going to use."

"Marvelous idea." Alex looked deeply skeptical at his abilities to provide her with food. She smirked. "If you come back empty-handed, I suppose we can always have peanut-butter-and-jelly sandwiches."

"Oh, you of little faith." Daniel heard the ping indicating that he had a new email and leaned forward to check the screen. He read the subject line and released an annoyed groan.

"Problem? Can I peek?" she asked. He nodded, her legs tangling with his bare ones as she leaned forward to look at the screen. He smiled at her squint.

"Do you need glasses to read, Lex?"

"Bite me." Lex cheerfully responded before frowning. "'Please date me.'" She read out the subject line for an email. There were more, some more direct than others. "'I'm your soul mate. I think I may be in love with you. I have really big…'" Alex's laughing eyes met his. "Did you register for a dating site or something? Or place an ad for a date on some skanky message board?"

Daniel glared at her. "No, that's the response from that article Grandmother made me do to promote the auction, and what it's like being one of the state's most eligible bachelors."

Alex giggled. "Oh my. This one says she's a bit of a nymphomaniac. How on earth did they get your email address?"

"They printed the ranch's website address. The public can email the ranch through the website. As they did." He gestured to the screen and grimaced. "Repeatedly."

Alex peered at the screen again. "Hey, this one is from a guy. The subject line mentions that the two of you have a mutual acquaintance."

"Not interested." Daniel leaned forward, highlighted all the offending emails and deleted them in one swift move. There was only one woman he wanted, and she was sitting next to him, driving him insane.

Daniel closed the lid of the laptop and stood up. Putting his hands on Alex's hips, he gently lifted her off the desk. But after placing her on her feet, he didn't—couldn't—let her go. How could he? She smelled like expensive soap and sunscreen, and her upturned mouth looked soft and inviting. Too much temptation—he had to kiss her, taste her. It had been so damn long.

Daniel threaded his fingers through her soft, upswept hair and held the back of her head as he covered her lips with his, keeping his kiss gentle, exploratory. It would be so easy to fall into heat and passion, but he didn't want to scare her. He just wanted to kiss her in the sunlight, skim her body with his fingers, be with her in this moment with only the blue sea and the hot sun as witnesses.

She tasted like coffee and spearmint and sexy woman, a combination that made his head swim. Daniel skimmed her rib cage, brushed his knuckles over her waist and laid his palm possessively over her stomach, his hand almost covering her from hip to hip. Pulling his head back, he looked down and emotion tightened his throat.

He pushed the words out. "Somewhere in there is my baby."

Alex's big smile was a kick to his heart. She lifted her hand and pushed back that annoying curl that always fell down his forehead. "I hope our baby has your beautiful eyes."

"I hope he has yours," Daniel whispered back. "You are so lovely, Lex."

"You're not too bad yourself, cowboy," Alex murmured, her lips moving against his. Daniel sucked in his breath as her breasts pushed into his chest. Then Alex pulled away and Daniel felt her arms tightening around his neck as her nose burrowed into the side of his throat. He barely heard her words, but somehow they still lodged in his soul. "Having a baby is scary, Dan."

"I know, sweetheart. But I'm here with you, for you."

Alex pulled back and he noticed the brilliant sheen in her eyes. He cradled her face and tipped his head to the side. "Why the tears, Lex?"

"If you are going to leave me, Dan, do it now. Before it hurts too much."

Leave her? His child? No chance. "I'm not going anywhere, Lex. I promise."

Alex forced a laugh before stepping back to wipe her eyes with the heels of her hands. She sent him a smile that was part embarrassment, part fear. "Ignore me. That's just hormones."

He nodded to give her an out, to allow her to walk away with her pride intact, but he knew that outburst had nothing to do with pregnancy hormones and everything to do with her fear of him disappointing her. Again.

Didn't she know that he would give her everything he was able to? His time, his support, his money, all his effort. Except his heart. He wouldn't give her that roughed-up organ. He liked it right where it was, thank you very much.

Daniel was either a very competent fisherman or the lady fish simply flung themselves onto his spear, thrilled to be caught by such a luscious merman. Alex was convinced the latter was true because they'd been eating from the ocean a lot lately, including tonight's dinner of a lobster salad. She could easily imagine the below-the-waves conversation:

Yes, Daniel, of course I will sacrifice myself for your eating pleasure.

No, take me.

He's mine to die for.

"What are you smiling about?" Daniel asked.

"I'm imagining a lady lobster's last words," Alex confessed, sitting down in the chair he pulled out for her. She was a modern girl, living a modern life, but she never tired of being the recipient of his gentlemanly manners.

"You are very weird," Daniel commented as he took his seat to the right of her. He reached for the bottle of white wine in the middle of the table and twisted the bottle to show her the label. "I found this in the cellar. It's nonalcoholic. Would you like some?"

"Drinking nonalcoholic wine is like drinking coffee with no caffeine," Alex grumbled.

Ignoring her, Daniel merely lifted a brow. Alex pushed her crystal wine goblet toward him. "Oh okay, then."

His mouth twitched as he poured the wine. Or, more accurately, grape juice. Alex gestured to the food. "Thank you for preparing dinner again. You're spoiling me. It's going to be difficult going back to Houston and having to look after myself. I've been living in the lap of luxury at the Lone Wolf and now here, with you. Real life is going to be a bit of a shock."

Daniel handed her a glass of wine and lifted his beer bottle in a silent toast. Alex sipped her wine—not too shabby, as it tasted like a decent chardonnay—and watched him in the low light, courtesy of the single candle between them and the firepits dotted around the pool. She sighed. How could she *not* look at him? They were on a private island in the Caribbean, her surroundings were absolutely exquisite, but still they paled in comparison to Daniel.

Graceful but masculine, mysterious and sexy with a thick layer of smart. His body was a masterpiece, and she could literally gaze at that face forever. She craved to hear his laughter fill the air, his lips drawing patterns on her skin. She wanted him. She would for the rest of her life.

And that was why she'd mentioned Houston, spoke about life after Galloway Cove. Because she needed a reminder that having Daniel in her life on a full-time basis was impossible. Deep down she knew this, and she couldn't allow herself to be seduced by a hot man who cooked for her.

She wasn't that weak.

Okay, she *was*, but wasn't identifying the problem the first step to finding the solution?

Daniel, bless him, helped her pull herself together by changing the topic to one she expected. "Tell me about your job offer."

She could talk about work—it was a nice, neutral topic of conversation. "Mike and I joined the company I still work for shortly after we left college. He left about six months ago to start his own business. He's asked me to join him—"

"This is in PR?"

Alex wrinkled her nose. "We don't handle public relations in a traditional sense. I specialize in creating social media strategies that best display and promote a brand or a company's image in the digital space."

Daniel grimaced. "Sounds like hell."

She flashed him a quick smile. "It would to someone who has absolutely no social media presence."

Daniel smiled at her and her stomach flipped over. "You stalking me, Slade?"

She'd never admit that in a thousand years. "I cyberstalk lots of people. But you should be embarrassed that your grandmother is very active on social media and you are not."

"Yet I'm not embarrassed." Daniel reached for the lobster salad and the serving utensil. He spooned food onto the plate in front of Alex before dishing up his own food.

"And this guy, Mike, wants to give you a partnership," Daniel asked, returning to the subject at hand. "Why would he do that?"

Alex forked up some lobster and groaned when the creamy sweetness hit her taste buds. Midchew, a thought hit her and she gripped Daniel's arm, her nails digging into the exposed muscle beneath his rolled up shirt sleeve.

"Problem?"

"I don't know if I should be eating shellfish," Alex said, pulling a face. "I think I read something about it not being safe for pregnant women."

Surely that was an old wives' tale. How could she be expected to walk away from all that bright, tasty, luscious salad? Resisting Daniel was hard enough, and now life was throwing another temptation in her way? Two words.

So unfair.

"I checked and it's safe to eat during pregnancy as long as its fresh and properly cooked. I caught and cooked it, and it's fine." Daniel waved his fork at her plate. "Eat."

Alex felt touched that he'd checked. It had been a long time since she felt protected, cosseted, fussed over. It was a nice feeling but dangerous. She couldn't allow herself to get used to being the center of any man's attention. Especially since that attention, along with love and respect and commitment, had the tendency to vaporize.

"You were telling me about Houston," Daniel prompted, leaning back and picking up his bottle of beer.

"Mike loves dealing with the clients—he's a born salesman but he's not so fond of overseeing the staff or paperwork. And the financial aspects of running a business. He's offered me a full partnership if I take over that side of the business."

Daniel looked out into the inky darkness. Alex followed his gaze and could just make out the boulders on the beach, the white bubbles of waves hitting the shoreline. "And you have to be in Houston to do that?"

Initially, Mike had suggested that she could spend the bulk of her time in Royal, commuting to Houston only a few days a month. Theirs was a web-based business and there was little that couldn't be managed over email and by video calling. It was Alex who'd pushed to move to Houston, who'd felt the need to get away from Royal and a certain sexy cowboy.

Yeah, that plan had worked out so well.

"I think I should be in Houston," Alex said, keeping her voice low.

Daniel took a few more bites of his dinner before pushing his food away. He used his thumb to trace the lines of the bamboo place mat. "What the hell happened to us, Lex?"

"We had sex and I got pregnant."

Daniel ignored the sarcastic retort. "I mean… back then."

To her, it was simple. He'd chosen The Silver C and Rose over her. What was there to discuss?

Daniel's eyes met hers and she almost whimpered at the pain she saw in his depths. "I asked for a long-distance relationship when you went off to college.

You told me that it had to be all or nothing. Why? Why did you insist that my leaving was the only way I could prove that I loved you?"

"Because I needed you—I needed *someone*—to choose me, to make being with me the most important thing they could do."

Daniel sat up and linked his hands behind his head. "I needed to stay on The Silver C. I couldn't leave, Lex."

"No, you *wouldn't* leave. Rose said no, and you just did her bidding. You didn't fight for me, Daniel."

Alex pushed back her chair and stood up, taking her nonalcoholic wine over to the edge of the pool. She sat down and dipped her bare feet into the sun-warmed water and stared out to sea. The rising moon was the silver blue of a fish scale, the flash of an angel's wing. It was a night meant for passion, for making love in the sweet, fragrant air. It felt wrong to be opening old wounds under the light of a benevolent moon.

She heard Daniel crack open another bottle of beer and then he was sitting next to her, thigh to thigh, leg to leg, feet touching in the tepid water of the pool.

"I'm sorry I hurt you, Lex," Daniel said in a raspy voice, and Alex heard the sincerity in it.

"I just wanted you to come to college with me, Dan. To be somewhere else with me, away from our grandparents and their disapproval and their stupid feud. I wanted to see who we could be when we didn't have all of that hanging over us."

"I couldn't and wouldn't leave, Alex. And it wasn't because I didn't want to."

Alex pulled her thigh up onto the stone rim of the pool and pushed her hair off her forehead. Half facing him, she ran her hand down his arm until she found his fingers. His spread open in welcome and her hand was quickly enveloped by his. She took a breath, knowing that she shouldn't ask a question she wasn't completely sure she wanted the answer to. But she was going to anyway.

"Explain it to me, Dan, because I still can't work it out."

Daniel pulled her hand from his and leaned back, his hands behind him. He tipped his head up to look at the stars, and Alex knew that he was looking for his words. Instead of answering her question, he turned his head and swiped his lips across hers, his tongue sliding into her mouth. Alex instantly ignited, and she wound her arms around his neck, falling into his touch. How could he fire her up with just his mouth on hers, his big hand holding the back of her head, anchoring her to him?

God, he was a magnificent kisser...

He was also, she dimly realized, brilliant at avoiding the subject. Reluctantly, Alex pulled back and scooted a few inches from him. "Nope, I'm not going to be distracted, Clayton. Talk to me."

"I always envied you, you know," Daniel quietly

stated. "I know that you lost your parents when you were really young but, God, you had this family that was pretty damn awesome."

"How would you know that? I mean, thanks to the feud, it's not like we saw much of each other growing up."

"Before I came to live with Grandmother full-time, I saw you when I was visiting. At church, at the town parade, the cookout at the community center." A small smile touched Daniel's face. "And maybe I saw more of you than I should've..."

"Meaning?" Alex demanded.

Daniel lifted one powerful shoulder. "I used to sneak onto Slade land, head for the tree house and watch you and your brother." He grimaced. "I'm sorry, that sounds creepy as hell, but I was young and, I suppose, lonely. After I moved to The Silver C, I started at school and life became busy and I stopped sneaking onto Slade land."

"Until the day you came across me in the high meadow. You were trespassing."

Daniel's mouth twitched. "I was on Clayton land."

"You wish you were," Alex retorted, her voice holding no heat, because how could it? Memories washed over her, as sweet as that summer's day. They'd started arguing about who was trespassing and before they knew it, they were inching closer and then Daniel grabbed her hips and she his biceps, and their lips touched.

"And then you kissed me."

"You kissed me," Alex replied because she was expected to. Soft laughter followed their familiar argument and Alex dropped her forehead to rest it on Daniel's muscled shoulder. "We loved each other so much, Dan, but it vaporized. I don't understand how that happened."

Daniel moved his head so that he could kiss her hair. "You asked me to do the one thing I could not do. You told me that leaving was the only way I could prove my love and that you would only carry on loving me if I did what you asked."

Alex frowned. "I don't remember saying that."

"Trust me, I heard it. And then you made me choose, Alex."

"And you chose The Silver C."

"I did."

His easy agreement hurt, but for the first time since she was eighteen, Alex felt the need to push aside the pain and understand. Daniel wasn't a guy who was careless with people's feelings, and she wanted to know and understand what drove him back then.

And now.

She was having a child with the man, so she had the right to try to understand him.

"I have no idea who my father is. He left before I was born, or so my mother said. She also said that he left after I was born, so who the hell knows what's true? I was raised in apartments, in trailers, in rented rooms and, for one memorable month, a women's shelter."

Dan ran his hand through his thick hair, then over his face. This wasn't easy for him and Alex respected him for opening up.

"Life with my mother was a matter of measuring the depth of the trouble and debt we were in—sometimes it was nose-deep and we were about to drown, and sometimes it was only ankle-deep. But it was always there…and she created most of it."

Alex kept her eyes on his face, scared to move in case he had second thoughts and stopped talking. She schooled her features because she knew that sympathy would make him clam up as quickly as inane platitudes would.

Stay still, don't breathe and just listen, Slade.

"When Stephanie tired of me or couldn't cope, she'd send me to Grandmother at The Silver C. Or my grandmother would ask to have me. Either way, she had to pay to have me at The Silver C. I once tried to work out how much she paid my mom and I stopped counting after fifty thousand dollars."

A low whistle escaped.

"Yeah, my mom was a piece of work," Daniel said, his voice steady and unemotional. But Alex could see the pain in his eyes and noticed the tiniest tremble in his bottom lip. His mother's lack of maternal instinct and his father's lack of interest still had the power to hurt him, Alex realized.

"So yeah, I watched you and seeing you with your

family, with Sarah, I was envious of how much you were loved. How secure you felt." Daniel placed his hand on her thigh and skimmed the tips of his fingers across her knee. "That summer, I know that you argued with Gus, with Sarah—you were angry with them so often."

Of course she'd been angry with them, as well as with Daniel. She loved him, he loved her, they wanted to be together and they were being kept apart because of a stupid feud. At eighteen, it had been all about her and what she wanted, and to hell with anyone else.

Ashamed of herself, Alex lifted her hand and gently touched Daniel's jaw. "Why did you let me leave, Dan? Why did you let me go?"

"You needed to go and I needed to stay." Daniel lifted his hand to rub the back of his neck. "Grandmother wanted me to stay, to learn about The Silver C. It was going to be mine someday and I needed to learn the ropes. I assumed that leaving with you meant risking the land, my job, my inheritance."

Alex jerked back, angry. "She said that?"

"No, you're not listening. I said I *assumed* that. The truth was, I didn't want to leave Royal. I felt safe there—welcomed, protected."

"And I asked you to leave it, to risk it."

"In hindsight, I know that I used my assumption of my grandmother disinheriting me and her displeasure as an excuse, but I couldn't tell you that I—"

"That you loved The Silver C more than you loved me."

Daniel started to deny her words but then stopped talking and shook his head. "I don't know, Lex. Maybe. All I know for sure was that I didn't want to leave. But neither did I want to let you go. I was so hurt, confused, unable to tell you what I was feeling."

"And I wanted you to make the grand gesture, to prove that you loved me," Alex admitted hoarsely.

"Stephanie did that, all the time. If I did x, I loved her. If I did y, I didn't. As a child I was constantly re-assuring her of how much I loved her, tying myself up in a knot trying to please her. After I went to live with Grandmother, I swore I'd never allow anyone to use love as a weapon against me again."

And by linking his love to his actions, she'd done precisely that. Ironically, the one thing she needed was the very thing her couldn't give her. What a mess.

Alex closed her eyes, trying to keep the tears away. "We were so young, Dan, dealing with feel-ings far beyond our comfort zone."

"And a raging attraction. It was like God gave the keys to a Formula 1 car to an eight-year-old. We were bound to crash and burn."

Alex touched her stomach and gave him a wry grin. "And it's happening again."

Daniel pushed his hand under hers so that his palm lay across her stomach. He placed his lips against her temple before drawing back. "The one thing I know we can handle is our attraction to each other. We can be friends and lovers, Lex. Trust me on this."

He sounded so sure, but Alex was still convinced that that toxic combination had the potential to blow up and rip them apart. Alex made the mistake of looking into those eyes—more umber than chocolate tonight—and saw need and desire swirling within those dark depths. She felt herself yielding, relinquishing her grip on common sense.

I'm exposing myself—I know that I am—but Daniel needs me.

And God knew, Alex needed him. Because here, right now, Daniel was silently telling her that he chose her, that he wanted her in his arms, in his bed.

No, he more than wanted her—he craved her.

As she did him.

Alex leaned forward and stroked the pad of her thumb over his lower lip. "Take me to bed, Dan."

She heard his sigh of relief and then his body tensed again. "Are you sure? You said this wasn't a good idea."

She lifted her shoulders and let them drop. "It isn't. We haven't found a long-term solution, and we should do that, but not tonight, not right now."

Daniel followed her to her feet and loosely held her hips. "What do you want us to do tonight, Lex?"

"I want you to love me, Dan. As only you can."

Eight

Instead of entering the house, Daniel led Alex down the deck and into the master bedroom, through the open sliding doors.

At the foot of the bed, he stopped and cupped her face in his hands, his thumbs tenderly stroking her cheekbones. In this dark room containing shadows and secrets, Daniel realized that right here, right now, for as long as it may last, they were about to reignite their love affair.

There had never been anyone else like her, no one who captured his imagination as thoroughly as Alexis Slade did. Whether she was lying in a meadow, hair in two plaits, or standing on a stage, raising money for a worthwhile cause, or lying on his bed, she entranced him.

He wished he could say otherwise but that was what Alex did. Entranced and ensnared. How was he ever going to let her go?

But that was the problem for Royal. Here, he wasn't a Clayton with commitment issues and she wasn't a scared Slade. They were Dan and Lex, lovers.

"God, you are so beautiful, Alexis."

Alex smiled at the use of her full name; she knew he only used it when he was overcome by strong emotion. Unable to wait another moment to taste her, Dan dropped his head and, not trusting himself to go caveman on her, gently touched his lips to the corner of her mouth. *Such sexy lips*, he thought. He wanted them on his, moving over his skin, wrapped around his—

No, if he went there now, before he'd even started, he'd lose it. No, tonight was about Alex and how best he could show her how much he lov—*adored* her.

Alex released a long sigh. "Daniel. The way you make me feel…"

Daniel dropped his hands to caress her neck and sighed when her tongue traced the seam of his lips, asking for entrance. His small release of air allowed her to slip inside to touch his tongue, and he was lost—control was vanquished. Daniel released a deep groan and he placed his hands on her hips and boosted her up, grateful when her legs locked around his hips, bringing her hot core against his harder, desperate dick. Wrenching his mouth off hers, he sucked in a breath, telling himself to calm down, that they had all night, that this wasn't a onetime deal. He had time tonight, tomorrow and the day after next.

Would it be enough?

Would forever be enough?

And why was he thinking of forever if this was just flash-in-the-pan lust?

"Lean back, Lex," Daniel growled. Frustrated with himself, he pulled her shirt up her body.

"Let me help." Alex whipped her shirt off and unsnapped the front clasp of her bra, allowing the lacy garment to drop to the floor and his mouth to close around one watermelon-pink nipple. Laving it with his tongue, he pulled back to blow on the puckered bud, smiling as he noticed her tan line, the darker and white flesh. Alex groaned and pushed his head toward her other breast, and he was happy to lavish attention on that bud, as well. It gave him time to lecture his dick, to remind it to go slow, to take it easy.

This was about Lex; it would only ever be about Lex.

Daniel lowered Alex to the bed and bent over her to tug her jeans apart, to pull the battered fabric down her hips and over her pretty toes. Running a hand down her long thigh and shapely calf, he blew on her aqua-lace-covered mound, pleased at her aroused scent—sex and sea and sun. Two cords held the triangle in place and Daniel's impatience had his thumbs and fingers gripping the cord and twisting, easily snapping the thin fabric. He pulled the fabric away from her and stared down at her.

"You're pretty and perfect. And mine, Lexi. Right now, tonight, you're mine."

He saw her gasp of surprise, caught the flash of pleasure in her eyes.

Standing up, Daniel whipped his shirt off, pushed down his board shorts and looked down at his lover, the mother of his child, the woman who'd slid under his skin at eighteen and whom he'd never been able to dislodge.

Mine. Only mine.

Daniel looked at her face, expecting her attention to be on him, and he frowned when he noticed that she was looking past him. If she'd changed her mind, he'd punch a hole through that expensive wooden screen that separated the bedroom from the bathroom. Replacing it would cost him an arm and leg, but it would be worth it.

Daniel pressed his forehead against hers. "Lex? Do you want to stop?"

Instead of replying to his question, Lexi placed her hand on her heart and sat up. When she finally looked at him, Daniel realized that he could see the moon in her eyes.

Literally. The moon was in her eyes.

He turned slowly and his mouth dropped in astonishment. The moon was as wide as the sky and he thought that if he leaned off the deck, he could run his hand across its silvery surface.

It was blue and aqua and silver and white…and absolutely magnificent.

"Daniel, it's so lovely."

He looked back at Lexi and slowly shook his head. The moon couldn't hold a candle to her. She was more radiant, more entrancing than any Caribbean moon hanging outside their bedroom window.

He ran his hand over her shoulder, his finger burning when it met her sun-touched skin. "I need you, Lex."

Lexi smiled and his heart spun in his chest like a damn prima ballerina. "Can I have you and the moon?" she asked, her eyes darting from him to the view outside.

He touched her nipple and rolled it between his fingers, his erection swelling when her eyes clouded with desire. Then Lexi's hand encircled him and the world stopped turning. He felt a tremor shoot him and told himself that he couldn't plunge… He had to hold still.

Lexi's voice was soft but sure. "I want you and the moon, Dan."

Since his brain didn't operate without blood, which was plunging south, Daniel shook his head to indicate his confusion.

Lexi kneeled and sent him a sultry smile. "Come behind me, Daniel. I want you to hold me, cover me, envelop me, make me scream. And I want to watch the moon while we do that. It's going to be a memory I'll always treasure."

Daniel moved to kneel behind her, his hands stroking the length of her back before placing his hand on her stomach to pull her back, to tilt her hips up. Wrapping his arms around her, he slowly entered her, his eyes burning at the sheer perfection of this moment. His completing her completed him.

He moved, slow, sexy movements that raised them up and up, closer to that silver orb hanging in the sky. His every sense was amplified: he heard the wind in the trees and the waves hitting the sand. Lexi's smallest whimper, her sighs of pleasure, were loud in his ears. Her scent filled his nose and when she turned her neck to find his mouth, he caught her eyes and they were an intense shade of touched-with-moonlight blue.

Lodged deep inside her, Daniel felt the rush of warmth, felt her contract and allowed himself to caress the moon and grab the stars.

In the Royal Diner, Gus looked up from his biscuits and gravy and into Amanda Battle's lovely face. The owner of the diner was one of his favorite people and he stood up to drop a kiss onto her cheek. "Good morning, beautiful."

Amanda laughed. "Should you be flirting with me now that you are married, Gus Slade?"

"Just stating a fact, ma'am." Gus took his seat again and sent a grinning Rose a wink. How wonderful it was to see his wife relaxed and smiling, happy in her skin. He'd done that, Gus thought, feeling proud. He'd made her glow from the inside out.

Amanda turned to Rose and bussed his wife's cheek with her own. "It's so nice to see you, Miss Rose. Congratulations on your wedding. I'm so happy for you."

Rose thanked Amanda for her kind words and for refilling her coffee cup. Amanda passed the carafe of coffee on to a passing waitress and tipped her head to the side. "So, the latest gossip is that you two sent your grandkids off on a honeymoon in your place? Are you crazy? Do you know how beautiful Galloway Cove is?"

Rose poured some cream into her coffee. "Those two are like two mules fighting over a turnip."

Amanda laughed at Rose's pithy saying. "Have you heard from them?"

"They managed to find a computer and have been in contact." Gus finished his breakfast and wiped his lips with his napkin. "They both sent us polite, gentle thank-you notes—"

Amanda swatted his shoulder. "They did not!"

"No, they didn't," Gus admitted. "But neither have they, after three days, called to be picked up or, as far as we know, killed each other."

"They might kill us when they get back, though," Rose said, wrinkling her nose.

"They'll work it out," Amanda assured her. "Or at the very least, they might be mad for a while, but they'll come around. You're family and they love you."

Amanda turned at the sound of her chime and Gus followed her gaze to the front door. Amanda frowned at the tall, well-built man entering the diner, his sharp business suit at odds with the rest of the customers' more casual attire. Amanda turned her back on him and looked at Rose. "Miss Rose? That man—do you know him?"

Rose leaned to the side to look at the Latino man and Gus saw the flare of appreciation in her eyes. Yeah, yeah, he was good-looking, but she wore his ring now.

"Rosie…" he warned.

Rose flashed him an impudent grin and turned her attention back to Amanda. "He looks a bit familiar, but no, I don't know him. Why?"

"He was in here the other day, looking for you. I think someone gave him directions to The Silver C."

"Since the wedding, I've been staying with Gus at the Lone Wolf," Rose said, blushing.

They really had to work out where they were going to live on a permanent basis, Gus thought. Strangely, Rose seemed more at home in his house than she did in hers. He'd been on tenterhooks, waiting for Rose to suggest that he move into Ed's house and still didn't know how to respond—he didn't think an "over my cold dead body" would go down well—but Rose had yet to make the request. That being said, they needed a house that was theirs, one neither of them had to share with the ghosts of the past.

"I should go to The Silver C, check up on the work."

"Daniel's foreman is a good man and no doubt Daniel is issuing his orders from Galloway Cove." Gus stroked the inside of her wrist to reassure her. He tipped his head back in a subtle gesture to the stranger. "Do you want to see what he wants?"

Rose shrugged and then nodded. "I'm here. He's here. Might as well." Rose looked at Amanda and smiled. "Would you mind sending him our way, Amanda, honey?"

Amanda nodded and glided, graceful as ever, away. Gus turned in his seat as dark, flashing eyes snapped to them. Gus looked at him, instantly recognized those eyes—funny that Rose didn't—and sighed. Oh hell, this could be either very good or very bad. The man slid off his chair at the counter and walked over to him.

The man stopped by their table and Gus could feel the tension rolling off him. He primed himself, ready to jump up and defend his woman. He might be old, but his reflexes were still sharp. Nobody would ever be allowed to hurt his Rosie again.

"Ms. Clayton—"

"That's Mrs. Slade to you, son," Gus growled.

"My apologies." The man held out his hand to Rose, and Gus felt his temperature rise, when instead of shaking it like a good Texan would do, he lifted

Rose's knuckles to his lips. "My name is Hector Lamb and I believe I am—"

"Daniel's father." Rose snatched her hand out of his grip, leaned back and sliced and diced him with her laser-sharp eyes.

"Where the hell have you been and why are you only showing up now?"

At the top of the trail, Daniel stopped, turned and looked at her as if he were surprised to see her on his heels. "Are you sure you're pregnant?" he demanded, hands on his hips, his eyes shaded by the brim of a well-worn ball cap.

"What makes you say that?" Alex removed her own cap and wiped her forearm across her forehead before resettling the cap on her head. They were deep into the mini jungle that covered most of the island, and it was humid as hell on a rainy day. She couldn't wait to get to the swimming hole that was reputed to be at the end of this long trail.

"You aren't experiencing morning sickness, you haven't had any weird cravings, you haven't been moody," Daniel replied. "And you're still as slim as you always were…"

Admittedly, it was taking some time for her to show, but there were signs. "The band of these shorts is tight and my boobs are definitely bigger."

Daniel sent her a steady look but she caught the devilry in his eyes. He lifted his hands and placed them on her bikini-top-covered breasts. "I don't believe you. I have to check."

His thumbs immediately found her nipples and Alex tipped her head up to receive his kiss. Oh, she liked this Daniel, this relaxed, funny, thoughtful man. For the first time since she'd moved back to Royal, they were connected on both a mental and physical level, and yeah, they gelled.

Whenever they weren't making love—which seemed to happen morning, noon and night—they talked and laughed. They had their differences, but their value systems were the same, their priorities were in sync. Respect and independence of action and thought were important to them and family always came first.

Family came first. But by moving to Houston, striking out on her own, she was deliberately putting time and space between not only the baby and Daniel, but the baby and its grandparents, uncle and her friends. Was she making life harder for herself in her effort to protect herself?

Daniel broke the kiss, took her hand and they continued walking alongside each other until the path narrowed and she was forced to fall into step behind him. She didn't *have* to move to Houston; it wasn't a condition of the partnership.

Alex bit her lip and stared at the back of Daniel's head, her eyes tracing his broad shoulders, muscles rippling under the red T-shirt he wore. She'd traced those muscles with her tongue…

Wrenching her eyes off Daniel, she pulled her thoughts back. The point was, she had options. Or, deep breath now, she could also move in with Daniel and give this—whatever *this* was—a shot. They could be a couple, raise their child together, day in and day out. Alex sucked in her breath and placed her hand on her sternum as she waited for the wave of unease to pass through her. When it didn't, she tipped her head, surprised. Huh. So moving in with Daniel didn't scare her as much as it did a week ago.

Her heart skipped a beat. They didn't need to get married but they could make this work. They had fantastic sex, enjoyed each other's company, had the same priorities...

Of course she knew the risks involved. Back in Royal, they would have to deal with real life, two careers, a baby on the way, their grandparents and... stuff. The mundane and the boring and the tedious. And there was always the chance that Daniel would one day decide that this wasn't the life for him and, well, leave.

Could she cope with that? Would she be able to watch him walk away without her world falling apart? Yeah, it would hurt when—if—he left, but he might not.

Could she do this? Dare she take a chance on Daniel, on the life he was offering?

Alex could feel her heart racing, and a fine sheen of perspiration covered her forehead. Feeling her courage well up inside her, she started to speak, but no words came out.

How was she supposed to tell him she'd come to a decision without saying the words?

"Here we are."

Alex pulled her attention from her thoughts and looked around, her mouth falling open at the tall waterfall plunging into a pool below their feet. Flat boulders dotted the natural swimming hole, providing a perfectly flat surface to stretch out on, to soak up the sun's rays after a chilly dip in the pool.

"Awesome." Daniel walked down the path to the first boulder, dropped his backpack to the rock and kicked off his trainers. Whipping off his shirt, he dropped it at his feet and then shimmied out of his shorts. What was it with this man and his need to swim naked? Not that she was complaining but...

Daniel sent her a wicked smile. "Secluded. No one else here. No one to see me and you've—"

"Seen it all before," Alex said, completing his sentence.

"Strip and join me," Daniel suggested, waggling his eyebrows. Yeah, she could live with Daniel looking at her like he'd been waiting his whole life to make love to her in a pool at the bottom of a pretty waterfall. Heat and warmth rushed to that special place between her legs and her nipples pebbled with expectation.

Alex felt beautiful, desired and wanton. Daniel stood in front of her, utterly unselfconscious, the sun touching his tanned skin. The wind ruffled his jet-black curls, and as her eyes traveled over his impressive physique, his erection jerked as he hardened before her eyes.

Having such a masculine, focused man want her made Alex feel intensely feminine, immensely powerful. She was life, she carried life, a goddess of the glen.

Alex quickly stripped down and stood in front of her man, sighing when the sun's warm rays caressed her bare back and buttocks. She pushed her breasts into his chest before dragging her nipples across his skin, her hand lifting to encircle him, her thumb brushing the tip of his cock. Daniel groaned and pushed into her hand.

"Make love to me, Dan. Here, in the sun, on this rock. On our secluded island."

Daniel nodded and she had a moment's warning when his eyes glinted and his mouth twitched. Strong arms wrapped around her and then she was flying off the rock, hitting the freezing cold water with a heavy splash.

Alex spluttered, shivered and kicked her way to the surface to see Dan's wicked smile and laughing eyes.

"You are such a child," Alex told him, launching a wave of water into his face.

Daniel ducked, grabbed her and she instinctively wound her legs around his waist only to find out that cold water had absolutely no effect on his erection at all.

Well then. It seemed like a shame to waste it.

Nine

After making love, they swam some more until they realized it was past lunchtime and they were hungry. They dressed, Alex in her fuchsia bikini and Dan in his board shorts, and then they ate the sandwiches Alex had prepared earlier and polished off the apples they had also brought along.

Feeling relaxed, Daniel replaced the cap on his water bottle and, after rolling up his towel, lay on his back and tucked the towel beneath his head. Enjoying the sun, he opened one eye to look at Alex. "Come lie down with me."

Alex curled into his side, her head tucked under his chin. The gentle breeze blew a strand of hair across his mouth. He picked up her hair and tucked it behind her ear.

"Best forced holiday ever," Alex murmured, her fingers idly drawing patterns above his heart.

"Best holiday ever," Daniel corrected her. "I love spending time with you, honey. I always did."

Alex opened her mouth to speak but closed it again. She had something on her mind—he knew that she was toying with a decision. Did he dare to dream that she'd reconsidered her living arrangements, that their forced week away—yeah, yeah, thanks old-timers—had worked?

"What's going on in that beautiful head of yours, Lex?"

Alex took a while to answer. "That job I was offered... I could actually stay in Royal and still take the partnership."

Daniel forced himself to stay still, but inside he was leaping to his feet, punching his fist in the air. "Are you thinking of doing that?" he asked carefully.

"Maybe. I sort of allowed you to believe that I had to move to Houston to take the partnership. I could stay in Royal and work remotely, traveling a couple of times a month."

He wanted to sit up, to whoop with delight, but he knew he had to tread softly because Alex was like a skittish colt that needed careful handling. Which was okay—he could tiptoe with the best of them. As long as he got what he wanted in the end, he didn't care how he got there. And he wanted Alex. In his arms, his bed.

And in his life.

"I'm scared of starting something, because I'm terrified I could lose it."

Daniel turned her words over in his head, trying to make sense of her out-of-the-blue statement. Pulling his head back, he looked at her but her eyes remained closed. He ran his hand up her spine, keeping his touch light and comforting.

"Care to explain that, Lex?"

Alex sat up, crossed her legs and he pulled himself up, bending his knees and allowing his hand to dangle between them.

"I don't like being left, Daniel. It's happened too often, and I don't think I can do it again."

He thought he knew where she was going with this but asked her to explain anyway.

"As we discussed earlier, losing my parents when I was young was a sad time, but Gus and Sarah stepped in and I was okay. However, when I was twelve, I lost my best friend Gemma, too. I don't know if you remember her—she was a redhead?"

He had a vague memory of seeing the two girls together, but he remembered the town's grief at Gemma's death more than he remembered the child herself.

"I was devastated. I thought my world ended." Alex pushed her hair back over her shoulder. "I had friends at school but nobody I was close to. I didn't want another friend who could die on me. So I kept my thoughts and feelings to myself and Sarah became my best friend. Then, in a meadow, I met and kissed you and I felt my heart opening up, expanding, and it became so full of you. That summer, you were my everything and I thought I was your world."

Alex touched the tip of her tongue to her top lip and when she looked at him, Daniel noticed the tears in her eyes. "I know it sounds dramatic but losing you felt like losing Gemma again. But somehow it was worse because you weren't only my best friend but my lover. All I wanted you to do was to choose me, to stick with me."

He suddenly understood. "You were angry that your parents and Gemma and, later, Sarah left you. You felt abandoned."

He got it.

"But I'm not allowed to be angry with them because they didn't have a choice to stay or to go."

"But I had a choice and I didn't choose you."

Alex nodded and scratched her head above her ear. "Being all grown-up, I thought I could handle having a fling with you. I thought I would sleep with you and keep it light and fluffy. And I was okay when I called it quits. I mean, I missed you but I knew that I could live without you. I think it helped that we didn't make an emotional connection, that it was all about sex."

They didn't make that connection because they'd both been too damn scared to go there. They still were. "Anyway, as for our current predicament… It makes sense for us to be together, to live together, to raise our child together," Alex quietly stated.

Thank the baby Jesus…

"But it also doesn't."

Crap.

Daniel looked at her and waited for her to continue, conscious of his heart thudding in his chest. Where was she going with this? "Carry on, Lex. Tell me what you are thinking."

"I'm scared of moving in with you, falling for you and then having to deal with you leaving, whether that's by death or a woman or whatever life might throw my way."

She was worried that he might leave her for someone else? Yeah, that wasn't going to happen. Not now, not ever. Alex pulled her bottom lip between her teeth. "I'm scared, Dan. I'm scared to try this, terrified that it won't work. I'm scared that you will become the center of my world again and when the day comes for you to make a choice, it won't be me."

She was a lot stronger than she gave herself credit for. They were both strong people; they'd both, in their different ways, survived so much. They could handle this.

He had to touch her, so he used the tip of his index finger to stroke the inside of her wrist. "I know you're scared, sweetheart. But there's something more frightening than fear and that's regret."

Alex released a heavy sigh and lifted her shoulders in a tired shrug. He could see that she was feeling overwhelmed and out of her depth. So was he but his childhood of rolling with the punches had taught him to not make decisions when he was emotional, that it was always beneficial to step back and look at a situation with some distance.

As much as he wanted to install Alex in his house as soon as he got back to Royal, he needed to give her time to find her way back to him. It was going to be hard, when his instinct was to take control, but if he wanted a family—this family—he had to take it slow.

"Can you see yourself staying in Royal? Is that something you can do?"

Alex stared at the pool below them and it took all of Dan's patience to remain silent. Eventually she nodded her head. "Yeah, I think that's a decision I am comfortable making."

Thank God. Do not punch the air, Clayton. You are not a child. Daniel held himself still. *You still have work to do but, God, that was a massive hurdle overcome.* "Okay then. Good."

He put his hands on her knees and waited for her troubled eyes to meet his. "Lex, you don't need to make any more decisions today. Take some time, think it through."

Alex bit her bottom lip. "What if I'd decided to move to Houston?"

He pushed his hand through his hair and met her eyes. "I don't know, Alex. It would've been more complicated, financially and logistically. But I like to think that we would've made it work."

Daniel prayed that she wouldn't pursue this line of questioning, that she wouldn't ask whether he would've moved to Houston and left The Silver C. Maybe. Possibly. Yes. But admitting that was a step too far. He was opening the door to his heart a bit too wide. Alex needed time and so did he.

"Rose and Grandpa are going to pressure us to get married," Alex said, directing her words to the pond and refusing to meet his eyes.

The last time he asked, she almost drew blood, her reply had been so cutting. "Do you want to get married?"

Alex shook her head. "I'm still coming to terms with my decision to stay in Royal. I can't think much beyond that. But, Lord, the gossip!"

"You speak as if the Claytons and the Slades haven't been gossiped about before," Daniel said, his tone wry. "Let them talk, Alex. We're working on our timeline, no one else's. We only have to answer to each other, nobody else."

Alex lifted her eyebrows. "Have you met our grandparents?"

He smiled at her quip but shook his head. "We don't have to be in a rush to figure this out. Let's take it step by step, day by day. Today you decided to stay in Royal—let that be enough for now."

Alex looked down at her hands before her deep blue eyes met his. "Okay. But I have one request."

Didn't she realize that he'd give her anything he could. "What, sweetheart?"

"I don't do well when there's no communication, when I think I am drifting on the wind. I need to be able to talk to you and you to talk to me. I feel better when we talk, when we have these conversations. I might not have the answers, but I don't feel so alone."

Touched beyond measure, Daniel clasped her neck with his hand and leaned forward to kiss her forehead. He'd watched her as a child, kissed her as a girl but this woman next to him? She was phenomenal.

"Do you know how many boys named Daniel were born in the greater Dallas area in '91?"

Rose looked from her kitchen at The Silver C to the informal dining table in the open-plan entertainment area and caught Gus's eye. How handsome he looked, she thought. How lucky she was to be married to him.

"How many?" Gus asked Hector Lamb, pushing the bottle of red wine in his direction. The red wine came from Ed's cellar. He'd collected the expensive wines because he thought it a classy thing to do but never drank the stuff. He'd never allowed anyone else to drink his collection, either. In the years since his death, Rose had sold the more collectible bottles and given away other bottles as gifts. She intended to drink the rest.

Rose pulled the cheesecake out of the fridge and looked around her immaculate kitchen. It was large and spacious and far too big for her and Gus. On the fridge was a magnet Ed had brought back from New York City, inside that drawer were his steak knives. She kept the flour in the same canister his mother did, the sugar in another. The windows were too small, the storage space badly designed.

Rose yanked open the second drawer and cursed when it became stuck before it was fully out. She was sick of sticky drawers and old furniture and poky rooms. She hated this house and was finally in a place where she could admit to it.

"Five thousand six hundred and sixty-two little boys were born during September and October of that year," Hector replied. "I knew the dates when Stephanie and I slept together—it happened over a week, so I gave Stephanie a little leeway in case the baby decided to be late."

Daniel was, in fact, early. "Hold on, boys, I want to hear how you tracked Daniel down," Rose told them, expertly slicing even portions of cheesecake. She scowled down at the half-cut dessert. When had she become so pedantic, so perfectionistic, so boring?

Rose defiantly cut the cake up into oddly shaped, differently sized pieces and wrinkled her nose. That didn't make her feel any better. She knew exactly what would…

After picking up the cake and three side plates, she walked over to the table and banged the cake down in the center of the table. She darted a quick glance at Hector before dropping an openmouthed kiss on Gus's lips.

Gus looked at her, shocked. No wonder. Regal Rose never ever engaged in public displays of affection.

"Are you okay, darlin'?" Gus drawled, surprise quickly turning to concern.

Rose nodded. "I hate this house."

Gus leaned back in his chair, rested his hands across his still-flat stomach and lifted his heavy gray eyebrows. "Do you now?"

"I don't want to live here anymore."

Hector cleared his throat and pushed his chair back. "Excuse me, please. I need to visit your bathroom."

Rose smiled, grateful to be able to speak to Gus alone. "Hurry back, Hector. This won't take long."

Hector nodded and walked away from them to the powder room just off the hall. Rose sat down next to him and placed her chin in the palm of her hand.

Gus smiled at her, a sweet, slow smile that was part devil, all charm. "Now, where are you wanting to live, Rosie? With me? My wife might have something to say about that."

She knew he was teasing but she was too nervous to smile. He'd adored Sarah. How was he going to react to her suggestion?

"You can tell me anything, Rose."

"I want to move into Sarah's house. I feel at home there, like she would be happy I was there, happy that I made you happy."

Gus's hands covered hers. "She missed you so much, Rose."

"I know. I missed her, too." Gus's wife, Sarah, had been her closest friend and Rose didn't know if she'd ever forgive herself for walking away from Gus and her best friend, the two people who knew and loved her best. How stupid young people could be! And that was why she felt no compunction in meddling in Daniel's and Alex's lives. If they couldn't see the wood for the trees, she'd damn well provide them with glasses and a chainsaw.

She had more to say and she might as well get it all out there. "I'd like Alex and her brother to choose what pieces of Sarah's furniture they'd like, and if there's anything special of hers you'd like to keep, I'd understand but—"

"But?" Gus asked gently.

"But I'd like a house of my own. I inherited most of everything that's in this home from my parents and great-grandparents and Ed didn't see the point of buying new when old worked as well as new." She was being silly but maybe Gus would understand. "I want my own stuff, Gus, new stuff. *Our* stuff."

Gus nodded once. "Then that's what we shall do, darlin'. And maybe Daniel and Alex can move in here. Alex will want to renovate and redecorate, do all that stuff new wives want to do but old wives don't let happen."

Rose grinned. Hearing Hector approaching her, she turned her attention back to him and smiled. "I am so sorry. We've been so rude. Tell us how you tracked down Daniel. And why did it take you so long?"

Alex looked out of the window of the private jet and saw the familiar landscape of Texas thousands of feet below her. In a half hour they'd be on the ground, and she and Daniel would be hurtled back into real life.

Dammit.

Real life meant deadlines and doctor's appointments, conversations with Gus and Rose, meetings with Mike. Real life wasn't lazy mornings, waking up tangled in Daniel's arms, listening to the sound of gently lapping waves and a gentle, fragrant breeze blowing across her skin. Real life wasn't fresh fish caught straight from the ocean, skinny-dipping in the cove or in the pool, making love in the outdoor shower.

Real life was grown-up life and she wasn't ready for it. On the island it seemed a lot easier to imagine staying in Royal, commuting to Houston for work, creating a life with Daniel. Now, a half hour out from that life, Alex once again questioned whether staying in Royal was the right option for her and her child. Was she taking too big a risk believing that she and Daniel could make this work?

Had she been seduced by spectacular sex on a sun-kissed island?

Alex drummed her fingers on the leather-covered armrest of her seat and gnawed her bottom lip, wishing that Daniel would look up, see her nervousness and say something, anything, to reassure her. But ten minutes after leaving Galloway Cove, he'd connected his cell phone to the in-flight Wi-Fi and hadn't stopped working since.

"Dammit to hell and back," Daniel muttered.

At least he was talking to her. Sort of. "Problem?"

Daniel lifted his head and grimaced. "More responses to that interview I did on being one of the state's most eligible bachelors. I have a thousand emails asking for a date."

"A thousand, really?" Alex asked, skeptical. He was a hot, sexy guy and there were a lot of desperate, lonely women out there, but that had to be an exaggeration.

Daniel turned the phone toward her and she saw the stream of emails on his screen. Okay, there were a *lot* of emails. "I thought you were picking up emails on the island, so why didn't you see these then?"

Daniel looked down at the screen again. It took him a while to answer as his finger flew over the small keyboard. "After deleting that first batch, I only checked my private email account on the island. This one is more of a general and PR account." He flashed her a quick grin. "I've opened a few emails and a couple of women did make a contribution to your charity to bribe me to date them."

Sex sold and, dammit, Daniel was sex on a stick. Alex tipped her head to the side and looked at him, dressed in his white button-down shirt and khaki pants, designer sunglasses hanging off his shirt pocket. If he ever became sick of being a cowboy/businessman, he could find another career as a male model. She could easily see him diving off a cliff, into a blue sea, swimming up to a boat and crawling all over a sexy, skinny model...

Modeling... Hmm...maybe next year she could do a skin calendar featuring Daniel and all the sexy, sexy men of the Texas Cattleman's Club. God knew there were a bunch of them.

Daniel narrowed his eyes at her. "No. Whatever you are thinking, just no."

Alex just smiled and didn't bother to argue. When the time came, she'd have him posing naked, maybe against a tractor or one of his fantastic quarterback horses, his Stetson covering his essential bits.

"Forget it, Slade," Daniel muttered, now looking nervous.

Alex handed him a coy smile and glanced at her watch. "So, what are your plans for today?"

Daniel tapped his index finger against his thigh. "I need to catch up with my foreman, get my PA to reschedule some meetings I missed, return calls. You?"

"Pretty much the same. Except that I am scheduling some time to kill my grandpa."

Daniel laughed. "Come on, honey, I thought we'd partially forgiven them. After all, we are back together."

What did that mean? Was she now his girlfriend, his partner, his lover? Alex looked out of the window as the plane started to descend. They'd only spoken in general terms about her staying in Royal… Did he still want her to move in? Was she supposed to look for a house to rent in Royal itself? What did they tell Gus and Rose?

Where, exactly, did they stand?

All she knew for sure was that she'd agreed to stay in Royal. Was she sure that was the right thing to do? For her and the baby…?

The baby. Alex frowned. "What's the date today?"

Daniel tossed out the date and she slapped her hand against her forehead. "Dammit, I nearly forgot that I have an appointment with the ob-gyn this afternoon."

"This afternoon?" Daniel demanded. "Didn't I put that into my calendar?" he glanced at his cell phone and nodded. "Yeah, here it is, five thirty."

Alex nodded. "She's fitting me in as her last patient of the day."

He sighed, ran a hand across his face and glanced down at his phone. He quietly cursed. "Can you reschedule? I've got a crazy day."

"I don't think I should. I should've seen her already and I won't be able to get an appointment for another two weeks if I miss this one," Alex told him. She lifted her hands and lied. "I can go on my own— it's not that big a deal."

"It's a very big deal and I told you I want to be there," Daniel retorted. "Today is just not a good day."

"I can't help that," Alex pushed back, becoming annoyed herself. "When I made this appointment, I didn't know we were going to be kidnapped and out of touch for a week."

Daniel scrubbed his hand over his face before speaking again. "Okay, let's calm down. You said the appointment is at five thirty? Where?"

Alex gave him the doctor's address before adding, "I'll understand if you can't make it, Daniel." Well, she'd try to understand.

Daniel leaned forward and covered her hand with his. "I said that I'd make you and the baby a priority, Lex, and I mean it. It would help if I could meet you there."

Alex linked her fingers in his and squeezed. She felt the warmth his words created and instantly relaxed. This was going to be okay; *they* were going to be okay. "Sure, we can do that."

Daniel leaned forward, brushed his mouth against hers and smiled. "Ready to go home?"

Alex smiled against his mouth. "No."

"Me neither. And please don't kill Gus. Prison orange is not your color."

Ten

Much later that day, Daniel gripped the bridge of his nose and closed his eyes. A headache pounded at the back of his skull and his shoulders were flirting with his ears.

It felt like he'd been back in Royal eight months instead of eight hours and he didn't know if he could fight another fire. He had cattle missing, he'd had to call the vet for a sick mare and one of his best men—who also happened to be one of his most experienced hands—had suddenly decided to retire.

On top of all of that, his PA had a stack of messages he needed to return, he had a pile of checks to sign and his accountant needed to speak with him urgently. Damn. He needed another vacation. But more than that, he needed Alex. Needed to see her smile, hear her voice.

Daniel looked at his watch. It was four twenty, which mean he'd need to leave the ranch by five to be on time for Alex's doctor's appointment. An image of Lex, rounded and beautiful, carrying his baby, flashed through his mind. He smiled. His woman was staying in Royal and in a few months' time, he'd meet the first of what he hoped would be a few children they'd make together.

Daniel heard the knock on his office door, jarring him from his thoughts, and looked up to see his grandmother's face between the frame and the door itself. He forced himself to keep his face blank, refusing to allow her the satisfaction of knowing her plan had worked out. Sort of.

"Can I come in?"

Daniel folded his arms as Rose stepped into the room. She looked good, he thought, and content. He liked seeing her happy but dammit, he wasn't going to smile at her...yet. "I'm not happy with you."

Rose didn't look even a little intimidated. "I don't care. I did what I needed to do."

Daniel spread his arms open. "Do I look like a little boy who needed your help?"

"You looked like a man who was going to allow the best thing in your life walk away from you." Rose walked over to his desk and placed her hands on the back of a visitor's chair. "I was not going to let her and that baby walk out of your life. And ours."

He couldn't help the smile that lifted the corners of his lips. "Be honest, you just want to dote on the baby."

Rose's smile made her look fifteen years younger. "I *so* do." She bit her lip and looked up at him, her eyes luminous. "So how did it go?"

Daniel smiled. "Do you use that look on Gus? Does he just fall at your feet and agree to anything you ask?"

"Of course he does," Rose replied. Daniel laughed and Rose surprised him by walking around the desk and winding her arms around his waist. He knew Rose loved him, but she wasn't given to spontaneous bursts of affection. Closing his eyes, Daniel gathered his grandmother close, resting his chin in her hair. This woman had been his rock and his safety net, his moral compass and his true north. He might not have had a father or much of a mother, but she'd filled the gaps with her no-nonsense attitude and her integrity. And her love. She wasn't a hugger but he'd always known that he was loved.

But yeah, he was going to hug the hell out of his kid.

Daniel dropped a kiss on Rose's head and started to step away. He frowned when his grandmother's arms tightened to keep him in place. "Gran? Everything okay?"

Rose stepped back and he was shocked to see tears on her face. Bending so that he could see into her eyes, he gently held her biceps. "Are you okay?

Is Gus okay? Did something happen? Crap, something has happened! Alex, is she okay?"

"Alex is fine, darling." Rose smiled and waved
her hands in front of her face. "Do you have a handkerchief?"

Who used those anymore? Daniel cast an eye
over his desk, saw a marginally clean bandanna
and scooped it up. He found the cleanest corner and
gently wiped away Rose's tears. "What's going on,
Gran?"

Rose held his hand and led him to the leather
couch that stood against the far wall. Daniel waited
for her to sit before taking the seat next to her. Rose
immediately took his hand in both of hers.

A million butterflies in his stomach started to beat
their wings. What the hell was going on? "Okay, you
are starting to scare me."

Rose stared down at his hands before releasing a
sigh. "Have you checked your emails lately?"

Weird question. "I've been keeping up-to-date,
mostly on my private email account. I glanced at the
emails on the general account and now know that
there are a lot of desperate women in Texas. Who
sends an email asking a perfect stranger out on a
date just because they read an article about him in
a magazine?"

"Lonely girls who want to marry a good-looking,
rich cowboy. You're a real-life fantasy."

Daniel snorted his disagreement. The only person he wanted to fantasize about him was Alex. The

thought of Alex reminded him that he had to get this conversation moving or he'd be late. "What's your point, Gran?"

"You might have missed it but there have been a couple of messages to you from a Hector Lamb."

Hector Lamb? He recognized that name. "Did he send me a message on the ranch account, saying he wanted to meet me to discuss a mutual acquaintance?" The butterflies started to take flight. "I presume he is talking about Stephanie."

Rose nodded.

Daniel ran a hand across the back of his neck. "What does he want? Does he know that we haven't had any contact with her since I was a kid?"

This wasn't the first time one of Stephanie's marks showed up at their door, demanding restitution. When he was younger, it had been a common enough occurrence—money frequently changed hands to keep Stephanie out of jail—but even after she broke off communications, there had been a few men who tried their luck trying to extort money from them.

"He doesn't want anything," Rose replied. "No, that's not true. He wants to meet you."

"Me? Why?"

Rose's eyes brimmed with tears again. "Hector was in Austin for business. He met your mom. They had a weeklong affair. He left and when he returned five months later, it was obvious that she was pregnant. Your mom told him that the baby was a boy, that it was his and that she was going to name him Daniel."

Daniel felt the room tilt, his vision go blurry. He forced himself to concentrate on Rose's words, to make some sort of sense of what she was saying.

"Stephanie was still married to her loser ex and she was using his name. Hector offered to look after her and his baby, and he returned to Houston to rent her a flat, to buy furniture and a car. She was supposed to arrive in Houston two weeks later but—"

"She never arrived."

"Because, you know, Stephanie could never make life easy for herself. She went back to using the name Clayton and Hector couldn't find her. More important, he couldn't find you."

Daniel forced the words out from between clenched teeth and dry lips. "He looked for me?"

"He never stopped." Rose's smile was gentle. "He saw that picture of you in that magazine article and just recognized you. He knew you were his."

"How?" Daniel croaked the word.

"You look just like him, darling. You couldn't be anyone else's child." Rose placed her hand on his shoulder. "Honey, you're trembling. I know it's a shock, but he wants to meet you, wants to know you."

Daniel scrubbed his hands over his face, his heart banging inside his chest. He took a couple of deep breaths before he remembered that parental attention and love always came with a price. Why was his father here? What did he want? What was in it for him?

And, crucially, how much was he prepared to pay to have his father in his life?

Rose's hand drew big circles on his back. "Do you want to meet him?"

He'd have to meet him to discover why he was here, what he wanted. "Yeah, I guess."

Rose's smile was pure delight. "Excellent!" She jumped to her feet and clapped her hands. "Because he's waiting at the main house with Gus. He wants to meet you, too."

Today? Now? Jesus…

Alex left the doctor's room, clutching a black-and-white picture of her baby, who looked—admittedly—more like a peanut than a baby. But the heart was beating strong, and everything, as the doctor had informed her, was progressing normally. She was as healthy as a horse and the baby was thriving. Could she come back in two months, and would the baby's father be joining her at future appointments?

Well, no. Because she was going to Houston, to start a new life there.

Alex looked up and down the street and glanced at her watch. Daniel had missed the appointment and was nearly two hours late. Obviously, she and the baby were not the priority he'd promised her they would be.

It was better, Alex told herself as she slid behind the wheel of her car, that she found out now and not later. She could still leave, she could wrench herself away from Daniel and Royal, and start afresh in Houston.

He didn't love her, and he would never put her first. They'd landed ten hours ago, and Daniel had already forgotten about her, forgotten that he'd promised to accompany her to this appointment. He'd looked her in the eye and told her that she and the baby were his top priority, that he'd put them first. It only took him ten hours to forget that promise, to put his work and The Silver C in front of her.

Alex felt the tears slipping down her face as she stared at the picture of their baby. Her heart cramped and she felt the familiar wave of uncertainty. Since breaking up with Daniel a decade ago, and reinforced by Sarah's death, she'd avoided emotional entanglements and this was why. Because she couldn't handle the disappointment, the fear and the uncertainty. Relationships made her needy, vulnerable and so very insecure. She'd spent so many years running away from those weak emotions, and by sleeping with Daniel, she'd opened herself up to them again. What a fool she'd been to think that they could raise this child together and that, maybe one day, she could trust him enough to build a future with him.

She couldn't even trust him to keep a damned appointment, so how could she trust him with her love, her feelings, her very scarred heart? No, it was better that she return to Houston, and in a few months, she'd contact him and make arrangements for him to be part of the baby's life. Hopefully by then, she'd be stronger and mentally together.

Her passenger door opened and a gust of cool, wet wind accompanied Daniel into the car. He slammed the door shut and fiddled under his seat for the lever to push the seat back. Leaning back, he stretched out his long legs as far as they would go before turning to face her, looking weary. "Hi. Sorry I'm so late."

Daniel rubbed his hands over his face as if to wake himself up before looking at her again. "How did it go? Are you okay? Is the baby okay?"

He was asking the right questions, but he sounded distracted, like he had more pressing problems on his mind. "God, it's cold out there."

Wow. He was talking about the weather. Could he not see that she was upset, that his missing the appointment had rocked her world? While Alex tried to make sense of his preoccupation—was he so oblivious that he couldn't see that she'd been crying?—Daniel reached for the sonograph. "Is this him? Her? Did they know what sex the baby is?" Okay, she now heard a little more interest in his voice. He cared about his child, that was obvious, but he hadn't cared to keep his commitment to her. She hadn't meant for it to be, but today turned out to be a test.

And he'd failed.

Daniel looked at her and frowned. "Are you okay?"

Well, no. "Do I look okay?" Alex asked, her voice soaked with emotion.

Daniel lifted his hand to touch her face and his expression hardened as she pulled back. "Look, I'm sorry I was late."

"You're not late, Daniel. You missed the entire appointment!"

"I know but—"

Alex banged her hand on the steering wheel. "No, no *buts*, Clayton! I asked you to be there, and you said you would."

"Something happened, Lex. If you'd just let me explain—"

She doubted that he could say anything that would make a difference. The fact of the matter was, once again, his precious ranch was more important to him than she was. "You believe that actions speak louder than words, Daniel. You told me this morning that I was your number one priority, that you would be here. Your actions disprove that."

Alex heard the frost in her voice, a direct contrast to the heat of Daniel's curse. She had to walk away—she couldn't do this for the rest of her life. She couldn't love him and not have him love her back. Great sex wasn't a good enough reason to stick around.

"Alex, for God's sake, let me explain."

She couldn't risk being persuaded to trust him, this would just happen again and again. Their time on the island had been a holiday romance, something that couldn't be replicated in real life. Real life wasn't sun and good sex and sparkling water; it was a chilly overcast day in Texas and two people who couldn't give each other what they needed. No, she had to end this today. *Now.* "I'm going back to Houston. That was my first instinct and I think it's the correct one."

"You're leaving Royal? Again? What the hell?"

Alex stared at the still-busy street, her eyes clear of tears. She was too hurt to cry, too empty to fight. She was in survival mode, simply doing what she could to emotionally survive.

"You're leaving because I missed one damn appointment?" Daniel's loud words reverberated through the interior of her car. "Are you completely insane?"

"No, I'm leaving because you can't keep your word! I'm leaving because I'm not a priority in your life and I can't trust you to be there for me!"

Daniel scrubbed his hand over his face. Looking up, he frowned at her, his dark eyes as cold as wind-battered boulders on an Arctic beach. "Jesus, Slade."

Alex gritted her teeth, leaned across him and opened his door. "Get out!"

Daniel pulled the door shut, leaned against the door and looked at her, his face now expressionless. She hated that blank look, the shutters in his eyes. Alex wanted to squirm under his penetrating gaze and forced herself to stay still, to lock stares with him. Daniel broke the heavy anger-charged silence. "You were just looking for a reason to run, weren't you?"

That wasn't fair. He was the one who'd let her

down, who hadn't stuck to his word. Alex tapped the picture of the peanut. "Funny, I didn't see you there when I listened to our child's heartbeat. I didn't hear you asking questions."

"If I made it today, then something else, soon, would've made you run," Daniel gritted out.

"That's not fair."

"Oh, it so is. When you get scared, you run as fast and as hard as you can."

His words were as sharp and as bitter as the tip of a poison dart.

"I'm not scared," Alex protested.

"You acted out of fear when, ten years ago, you ran instead of trying to find a way to still go to school and see me. We started sleeping together last year and as soon as we started laughing together, talking, you broke it off."

"Our grandparents—"

Daniel leaned forward, his face harsh. "Don't! Don't you dare blame this on them! This is about you and me and the fact that whenever you find yourself in deep water, emotionally speaking, you swim back to shore!"

That was because she didn't want to drown. She knew what it felt like to lose air, to feel like you were dying without the people you loved in your life.

Daniel shoved both hands into his hair and tugged his curls in frustration. "We could have such an amazing life, Lex, but you value protecting yourself above loving me, loving us." Daniel dropped his hands and, in his eyes, Alex saw the devastation she'd put there.

"I can't keep trying to prove my worth to you, Alexis. I did that constantly as a child and I refuse to do it as an adult. You either want us—me—or you don't. I'm not going to continuously try to prove myself to you." Daniel picked up the photograph of their baby and looked at it for a long time. "I'm tired of fighting for us on my own, Lex. I want you. I want my family, but I need you to want it, too. And I'm not going to sit here and beg you for that chance. Go back to Houston, live in your safe cave."

She heard the words, thought that was what she wanted, so why did it feel like he was ripping her soul in two? Daniel opened the door, swung his long legs out of her small car and looked at her over his shoulder. "I'll contact you in a few weeks to check up on my kid."

Daniel left those parting words behind as he exited her vehicle. To check up on his child, not her. She'd pushed him, and she'd got what she wanted. A Daniel-free life. Alex ran the tips of her fingers over her forehead, utterly confused. She felt like she'd placed the last piece into a giant puzzle only to find that the focal piece of the picture was missing. What had she missed?

Acting on instinct, she flew out of the car and saw him walking away, his shoulders hunched and his head bent. "Daniel!"

He stopped at her shout, hesitated and finally turned to face her, lifting a dark eyebrow. "What?"

Hold me. Take me in your arms and soothe my fears. Tell me that you'll never let me down. Never leave me. Love me, please.

"Why were you late?" she asked.

A small smile touched his mouth but didn't reach his eyes. "Oh, that little thing?" He hesitated, drawing the moment out. "A half hour before I was supposed to meet you, my father walked back into my life."

Eleven

The next morning, Daniel rested his forearms on the whitewashed pole fence and watched as one of his stable hands led Rufus, his prize stallion, from the barn to spend the day in the paddock behind his house.

Rufus had it made, Daniel thought. He and Rose and every other hand petted and pampered him and treated him like the king he was. Rufus got fed and brushed and stroked, and he could frolic and mate with a variety of mares.

Lucky Rufus. His life had certain parallels with his favorite horse. He thought he could go through life running his ranch, socializing with his friends and falling into the arms and bed of any available woman who caught his fancy. He thought that was living, but as it turned out, he hadn't had a clue.

Truth was, he wanted what he couldn't have. He wanted Alex, he wanted his child, he wanted a life together. Early-morning coffee in bed, long trail rides over the Clayton and Slade ranches, alone or with their child safe between his arms and knees. He wanted to walk into his house and see her there, watch her grow rounder and bigger, kiss her mouth when she brought their child into the world. He wanted to make dinner with her, listen to her read stories to their children, snuggle with her at night.

He wanted to love her body and nurture her soul.

He simply wanted the opportunity to love her.

Daniel scratched his forehead, his head pounding from sadness, stress and the half bottle of whiskey he'd consumed when he got home last night. He'd missed one appointment—and had a damn good reason for doing so—and she'd written him off as being untrustworthy, inconsiderate. She should've allowed him to explain and then decided, not jumped the gun. If he spoke to another woman, would she think he was having an affair? If he was a minute late, would he be in for a night of receiving the cold shoulder? He wasn't perfect; no man was, and Alex didn't seem to allow any room for him to maneuver.

He couldn't love someone who only loved you back when you proved your worth, who was only happy when you did what she wanted you to do. He loved Alex but he wanted a wife and a partner, not a shadow. He wanted a friend and a lover, not a prosecutor, cross-examining him on his every move.

Sighing, Daniel stared at the empty paddock. Maybe she was right, maybe they were better off apart. Maybe they'd been living in a fool's paradise while they were on vacation at Galloway Cove, allowing the fresh tropical breezes and the island's sultry allure to sway them into believing that they could have the impossible.

How many times were they supposed to try? Shouldn't he just accept that he and Alex were not meant to be?

"Morning."

Daniel turned to see Hector approaching him, dressed in an Italian suit. He looked down at his jeans and worn denim jacket over a flannel shirt and thought that while he and his father looked so alike, he didn't have Hector's taste in clothes.

"Hey."

Daniel hadn't had the chance to have a private moment with Hector, to take him aside and find out what he really wanted. The meeting at Rose and Gus's had carried on and on, and his grandmother had been less than pleased when he insisted that he had to go because he had a prior commitment that couldn't wait. Hoping to catch the tail end of Alex's appointment, he'd floored it to Royal, but he'd been too late.

And because he was late, his world had fallen apart.

"We didn't have time to have a one-on-one conversation last night," Hector said, coming to stand next to Daniel. "Your grandparents are extremely hospitable, and they love you very much."

"Rose is my grandmother. Gus is a new addition to the family," Daniel replied. Tired, upset and not wanting to indulge in small talk, he looked Hector in the eye. "What do you want?"

Shock passed over Hector's face before he schooled his features. "What do you mean?"

"Money? An introduction? A new sports car? A loan?"

Hector cocked his head to the side and instead of anger or annoyance or shame, Daniel saw sympathy in his eyes. "None of those."

"Well, what?" Daniel demanded, his voice ragged. Because there had to be a reason he was here, back in his life.

"I have more than enough money, and I don't need your connections. I own six sports cars and I am excessively liquid." Humor touched Hector's mouth. "But thank you for offering."

Daniel pushed a hand through his hair. "Then why are you here?"

Hector placed his hand on his shoulder and squeezed. "I am here because you are my son. I have three daughters with a lovely woman who has been my life for more than twenty-five years, but you are my firstborn, my son. I am here because I need to know that you are happy, healthy, okay. I also wanted you to know that I never stopped thinking about you, that I was always looking for you. There's no price to pay, Daniel."

Daniel stared at him, shocked. "What did you say?"

Hector sent him a soft smile. "I didn't spend much time with Stephanie, but it didn't take me long to work out that life was a series of exchanges with that one. Do this for me and I'll do this for you. Pay me this and I'll do that. Pay me more and I'll pretend to love you.

"Why do you think I was so determined to find you? Apart from the fact that you were mine, I didn't want your life being a series of transactions."

Oh God, that was exactly what life with Stephanie had been like.

Daniel felt like he needed to say something, anything. "I've always thought that was what love was. Up to now, it's all I've known. My grandmother married Ed to make sure her mother was cared for... Stephanie only allowed Gran to have me if she paid for the privilege." A muscle ticked in his jaw. "And then, of course, there's Alex. She dumped me ten years ago when I refused to leave The Silver C with her."

"She was a teenager and, as such, stupid," Hector said, his voice mild. "I'm sure you hurt her, as well."

He had. By refusing to leave The Silver C, choosing the ranch over her, he made her feel abandoned. To a girl who'd been left by so many people, she felt any loss more keenly than most people did. She'd been scared and was still scared…

So was he. When there was so much to lose, love was goddamn terrifying.

Earlier, instead of explaining, instead of reassuring her, he'd turned the tables on her, accusing her of wanting to run. Guilt coursed through him. Rather than trying to see things from her perspective, he'd cast blame, got angry. He'd been confused and upset about Hector dropping back into his life, worried that the man he instinctively liked would disappoint him by putting a price on fatherhood.

Driving to Royal, he remembered thinking that his life had been so much less complicated last year: he'd had affairs that had the emotional depth of a puddle, his grandmother wasn't in love with her oldest enemy and Alexis Slade was a girl he saw around town, whom he was determined to keep at arm's length.

His life had been safe. But, God, so boring.

He didn't want that. He wanted to watch his grandmother fuss over her new husband, and he wanted to get to know this man who'd looked for him for the better part of three decades. He wanted his woman, his child, the two most important things in his life.

Because while he loved this land, loved The Silver C, the *love of his life* was probably packing up her car and heading south.

Daniel looked at Hector and lifted his shoulders

and his hands. "I'm running out on you again but it's not because I want to, but…"

Hector smiled. "But there's a girl leaving, and you want to stop her."

Rose and her big mouth. Daniel smiled. "I intend to make that girl your daughter-in-law."

Hector grinned. "Sounds good to me." He pulled a card out of the top pocket of his suit and handed it to Daniel. "When you are ready, come to Houston, bring Alexis, meet my family. Or come alone, whatever…"

Daniel took the card and nodded once before scuffing his boot over the short dry grass. He cleared his throat, pushing down the emotion that threatened to strangle his words. "Thanks for looking for me."

Hector squeezed his shoulder again. "It's what fathers do. Go get your girl, son."

Son. Daniel heard the word and closed his eyes. He was finally someone's son. It felt good, wonderful. But it would be freakin' fantastic to be Alex's husband and the peanut's dad.

Alex recognized the sound of Gus's ancient ATV and wondered how much longer he'd continue to nurse that ancient beast. It sputtered and belched smoke and was in the shop for repairs more often than it was on the road. Gus had access to three brand-new ATVs a couple of steps from his front door but his loyalty to that old, paint-deprived quad bike remained constant.

Her grandfather was the most loyal of creatures.

He'd loved Sarah—of that she had no doubt—and he'd treated her like a queen, but when he was with Rose, he glowed. Her hard, tough, frank-as-hell grandfather was putty in Miss Rose's hands. He loved her to the depths of his soul, beyond time, for eternity.

Rose, she was surprised to find, seemed to love him just as much. Rose was now Gus's world and Alex was happy for him. Happy that he'd spend the rest of his life loving and being loved.

She couldn't help feeling a little envious, but she shrugged it away, thinking that love like that perhaps now only existed for people of a certain age, a particular generation. She and Daniel were modern people, living in a modern world, and they'd been conditioned to be selfish, to be self-obsessed. How could true love flourish in a society that was so materialistic, self-loving and narcissistic? It was all about them, only about them. She was a classic example because she'd been so caught up in her own drama, in thinking how badly Daniel had treated her in failing to make the doctor's appointment, that she'd brushed aside his explanations. *Her* feelings, *her* heartache had been all she'd been worried about.

Daniel meeting his dad had been a damn good excuse to miss her doctor's appointment, and if she hadn't reacted so selfishly, she might not be sitting in the chair on Sarah's deck, her car fueled and packed, ready to make the journey to Houston and a new life.

She was thoroughly ashamed of herself. And now,

more than anything, she wanted to know how he was dealing with his father's reappearance. What did Daniel think of his dad? Was the reality of meeting him as an adult as good as the dream he'd had of him as a boy? But no, because she'd acted like a selfish brat, he was dealing with this all alone.

Alex sighed as she heard Gus's footsteps on the wooden stairs that led to the tree house. Her grandfather's shadow fell over her and she lifted her head and greeted him. Gus nodded, dropped into the Adirondack chair next to her and propped his old boots on the railing. His pushed his ancient but favorite Stetson back with one finger like she'd seen him do a million times before. Old ATV, old boots, old Stetson, Rose.

The man never gave up on the things he loved. Alex bit her lip as the thought struck home. Gus didn't give up; few Slades ever did. So why was she?

Gus cleared his throat and Alex turned her head to look at his profile. "Do you remember when Gemma died?"

Alex jerked her head back, surprised at his question. That was the very last thing she expected him to say. "Sure. I remember getting the news. I thought my world had stopped."

"Do you remember the funeral?"

Alex shook her head. "Not so much, actually. I remember the coffin, the flowers, Sarah holding my hand."

Gus stared at the barren winter landscape beyond

the river. "We woke early that morning, the day of the funeral. Sarah looked into your room but you weren't there, and we couldn't find you. We looked everywhere. You never took your hound with you that day. You two were never apart and that scared me."

Olly had died in her arms only a few months later after being kicked by a horse. It had been another loss in a string of losses. "I eventually saddled a horse and told your dog to find you. We went for miles and I eventually found you in the top paddock, the one that borders the Clayton land."

The one where she first kissed Daniel. Yeah, she knew it well. "It was the farthest point you could go without crossing onto Clayton land, and you were standing right on the boundary line."

Alex tried to remember but nothing came back. "I don't remember any of this."

Gus rubbed the back of his neck. "You told me that you were running away, that you couldn't go back. That going back would make it too real."

That sounded like her.

Gus slid down the seat, rested his head on the back of the chair and closed his eyes. Alex waited for him to continue but he just sat there, soaking up the winter sun. She flicked his thigh and he cranked open one eye. "What?"

"Aren't you going to tell me that I run away from stuff I don't want to have to deal with? That I did it ten years ago when I left Daniel—"

"In fairness, I did encourage you to do that," Gus said, his eyes still closed.

"So why aren't you pointing out that running away is what I do, that it's the way I deal with life when things get hard? That I push people away when I think they can hurt me? Why aren't you telling me that?"

"You seem to be doing a right fine job working this out on your own, sweetheart. Seems to me that you don't need my input."

Alex glared at him before dropping her gaze to her hands, which were dangling between her thighs. Running, hiding, staying away—emotionally, as well as physically—was what she did. She dipped her toe in and yanked it out when the water got deeper, the current stronger. As Daniel suggested, she played in the shallows, too scared to take a chance.

"I'm so scared, Grandpa," Alex whispered, her voice so low, she wasn't sure he had heard her small admission.

"So?" Alex looked at him and he shrugged. "Be scared. Be whatever you need to be, but instead of running, be scared while you stand in one place, while you try something new." Gus stood up and pinned her to her chair with his don't-BS-me blue eyes. "I loved your grandmother, Alex. I really did. But a part of me always regretted walking away from Rose, for missing out on fifty years with her. Regret is a cold hard companion I don't want you to live with. Daniel is a good boy—"

Alex couldn't help putting her hand on her heart and feigning shock at his praise of a Clayton.

Gus blushed and waved her mockery away. "Yeah, yeah. But he is a good man—he's loyal and hard-working, and God knows you two burn hot enough to start a wildfire."

Alex grimaced. That wasn't something she wanted Gus noticing. Gus bent down to kiss her cheek. "Don't run this time, Lexi. Stay still and see what happens. Gotta go. Need to check on the calves in the stable paddock."

He had hands and Jason to do that for him, but Gus would ride back on the wheels-on-death because he wanted to. No, because he *needed* to. Alex watched the best man she knew walk away, his back still strong, his gait still steady. He was hard and tough and frank, but her grandfather had an enormous capacity for love. For his family, both present and past, for his land and for his beloved Rose. He'd lived and loved and cried on this land. He tended it and it repaid him by providing a good livelihood for his kids and grandkids. His beloved wife and children and pets were buried in the family graveyard, and every inch held a memory. The land was an intrinsic part of him, just as Clayton land was a part of Daniel.

And they belonged here. Both of them, on this land. Together.

It was time, Alex thought as she stood up, to put this latest, most stupid Clayton-Slade feud to bed.

* * *

Her car was filled to the brim and Alex knew that if anyone saw her driving it, they would immediately assume she was leaving Royal and the gossip would fly around town. She and Daniel had created enough gossip lately, so she decided to quickly unpack her vehicle before tracking down Daniel.

She wouldn't take all her worldly possessions back up to her room, as that would take far too long, so Alex decided to dump them in Gus's spacious hall until she returned. She parked her car as close as she could get to the front door of her childhood home, exited her car and walked around to the other side. She had a heavy box of books in her arms when she heard the low rumble of a powerful pickup. Turning, she squinted into the sun and saw the dusty white truck with The Silver C's logo on the side panel.

Alex held the box, conscious that her mouth was as dry, as Gus would say, as the heart of a haystack. Watching as the truck stopped next to hers, Alex stared wide-eyed as Daniel flew out of the car, his face radiating determination and a healthy dose of kick-ass. He was at her side in two seconds and then the heavy box was yanked out of her hands and tossed, with very little effort at all, into the back of his truck. The corner of the box hit a fence post and the box split open, spilling books over the bed of the truck.

Before she could protest, Daniel grabbed her biceps and slammed his mouth against hers in a hard kiss, but as Alex started to sink into the kiss, he whipped his mouth away. Holding her arms, he easily lifted her away from her spot by the door and grabbed a suitcase and a toiletry bag, tossing both into the bed of his pickup.

Since that was exactly where she wanted her stuff, Alex watched him, her shoulder pressed into the side of the car as he emptied her car in a matter of minutes. She wished he'd taken a little more care in moving her potted plants, but she was sure they'd be okay.

When her car was completely empty—Daniel had even chucked her bag and phone onto his passenger seat—he stormed back to her and placed his hands on his hips, his chest heaving.

"You are not going to Houston," he stated, his voice gruff.

She'd gathered that already. Alex just resisted throwing herself into his arms and it took everything she had to lift an insouciant eyebrow. "You kidnapping my stuff, Clayton?"

"I couldn't give a damn about your stuff," Daniel muttered. He jerked his head toward the pickup. "Get in."

There was something wonderful in seeing her man slightly unhinged, Alex thought. She was quite curious to see what he'd do if she dissented. "And if I don't?"

Alex expected him to toss her over his shoulder, to bundle her into his car, and she was turned on thinking about Daniel going caveman on her. But instead of utilizing his physical strength, he lifted his hand to gently touch her face. "I need you, Lex. Right now, I need you to get into my truck because I have things to say…"

"Like?"

Daniel rested his forehead on hers. "I want to tell you that I need you, period. In my bed, my house, my damned life. Nothing makes sense without you."

Alex turned her cheek into his hand, refusing to drop her eyes from his. This was Daniel, naked and exposed in a way she'd never seen him before. "We make sense, Alexis. We made sense ten years ago, but we were too young and dumb to know it. We made sense three months ago, but we were too scared to acknowledge it. You and I, we're two puzzle pieces that interlock. You're…"

Alex felt the moisture on her face, saw the sheen of emotion in his eyes. "What am I, Dan?"

Daniel held her face within both of his hands as her heart slowly slid from her chest to his. "You're everything, Lex. You're both my future and my past, my baby's mother and the beat of my heart. Please don't go to Houston. Stay here with me."

"Okay."

Daniel yanked his head back, a smile hitting his eyes with all the force of a meteor strike. "Are you being serious?"

Alex nodded. "When you roared up, driving like a crazy man, I was actually unpacking, not packing. I was coming to look for you."

Daniel's thumb skated over her cheek. "Why?"

Alex gripped his shirt, bunching the fabric in her hands. Preparing to jump, she gathered her courage. "I want to stay. I want to be here with you. Raising our children together."

More shock. Daniel looked down at her stomach and jerked his head up. "We're having twins?"

Alex laughed. "Not this time. I was talking about the future, the future I see with you."

"Damn. Twins would've been fun." He brushed her hair off her forehead, his expression tender. "How do you see our future, Lex?"

"Pretty much as you said earlier. I know that I have some issues, Dan, but I don't want to live my life fearing something that may not happen. I'd rather have any time I can have with you than no time at all. I'm not saying that I'm not going to be insecure, to worry. I probably will but I'll try not to be ridiculous about it."

"And instead of getting frustrated, I'll just hold you tighter and tell you that I'm never going to let you go."

He was gruff and bossy and powerful and sometimes annoying, but he was also perfect. She tipped her head back. "I love you, Daniel. I'm crazy in love with you."

Daniel's smile was pure tenderness. "I love you, too, sweetheart."

Alex's mouth lifted to meet his and she tasted love on his lips, relief in his touch, happiness dancing across his skin. She was feeling pretty damn amazing herself. The kiss deepened, became heated and Daniel pulled her into his hard body, chest to chest, groin to groin. Tongues tangled as love and belonging and desire merged into a sweet, messy ball. This was the start of a new chapter and Alex couldn't wait for the rest of the book.

Daniel's hand came up to cover her breast and it took all her willpower to pull away from his touch. She gestured to the busy stables to the left of the house, blushing when she saw Gus and Jason leaning against the wall, unabashedly watching them.

"Jerks," she muttered.

"On the plus side, I didn't get my head blown off," Daniel murmured, laughter coating his words.

"Actually, Grandpa quite likes you," Alex told him. "He'd like you more if you married me."

Daniel jerked back, frowned and then released a strangled laugh. "I'm not sure what to say to that." He rubbed his jaw. "How do you feel about that?"

"Getting married?" Alex cocked her head to the side, pretending to think. "I think that sounds like a fine idea." She grinned at his astonishment and held up her hand to keep him from grabbing her again. "Slow down, cowboy, I'm not getting engaged with tear tracks on my cheeks and blue rings around my eyes and with my male relatives watching us like hawks. But do feel free to propose in the high meadow, preferably with a lovely ring and a bottle of champagne."

Daniel pretended to consider her statement. "Hmm, the ring I can do. But it'll have to be non-alcoholic champagne, and whose land will it be on?" He smiled and Alex's heart flipped over.

"Ours," Alex said, the words catching in her throat. "Yours, mine, ours."

Daniel nodded, raw, unbridled emotion in his eyes and on his face and in his touch. Alex watched his eyes as he bent to kiss her, silently saying a heart-felt thank-you to whatever force had brought them to this point. They were going to have a hell of a life and she couldn't wait for it to start.

"Hey, you two, what's the status?" Alex jumped, startled, and she turned to see her Gus a few feet from them, waving his phone in the air. Since when did he carry a phone? Alex wondered. "Rosie wants to know."

Daniel gently banged his forehead on her collar-bone. "God."

"Everything is sorted," Alex told Gus, making a shooing movement with her hand.

"Rosie, let's hallelujah the county! Call everyone—we're going to paint the house. And the porch." Gus flipped his phone closed—so old she was surprised it still worked—caught Daniel's eye and gestured to the truck. "Well, come on, then. This stuff isn't going to move itself. Take it into the house and we can have a chat about what comes next."

The last thing she wanted to do was to talk to Gus, or anyone. What she really wanted to do was to divest Daniel of his clothes and make love to him as his future wife.

Daniel looked from her to his truck, adjusted his ball cap and shook his head. "As much as I appreciate the offer, sir, I'm going to stick to my original plan."

"And that was?" Alex asked as his hand enveloped hers.

"To kidnap you and your stuff." He flashed a grin at Gus as he wrapped an arm around her waist and easily carried her to his truck. He bundled her into the passenger seat and saluted Gus. "I try to learn from my elders, sir."

Epilogue

At six months pregnant, Alex required a wedding dress with an empire waistline but, catching a glance at her reflection in the gleaming glass door as she stepped out of the TCC function room, she saw that she still looked pretty amazing. The dress's bodice gathered into a knot behind her breasts and the chiffon overskirt, which was dotted with embroidered roses, flowed to the floor. She was, as everyone kept telling her, glowing. Alex knew that had as much to do with her husband of two hours as it did her pregnancy.

She was married. Alex looked down at the band of diamonds Dan had put on her ring finger earlier, a companion piece to her sapphire-and-diamond engagement ring, and took a moment to count her many blessings. Her partnership with Mike was smooth sailing, and while commuting was a pain, so far it was working. She was living in Dan's house and they were deciding how to completely renovate Rose's old house together. In Rose she found both a mentor, a friend and an ally. And in getting to know Sarah's oldest friend, she felt like she had a piece of her grandmother back.

Best of all, she woke up with Dan and fell asleep with him, secure that her heart was safe in his hands.

"Have I told you how stunning you look?"

Alex turned at her husband's voice and smiled. He didn't look too shabby himself, looking almost as hot in a tuxedo as he did in worn jeans and a T-shirt. But Daniel naked? Couldn't get sexier…

Daniel approached her, held the back of her head and tipped her chin up to brush her lips. "We haven't had a moment to ourselves since we walked into that church."

Their friends and family—including Daniel's father, his wife and his three half sisters and their spouses and many children—all wanted some time with the new bridal couple. While Alex appreciated their well wishes, her cheeks were sore from smiling, her feet ached and she just wanted to step into Daniel's arms for a cuddle.

"You doing okay?" Daniel asked, placing his hand on her round stomach.

"A little tired." Alex looped one arm around his

neck and rested her cheek on his chest. "I'm so thrilled that we are going back to Galloway Cove for our honeymoon, Dan. I just want you and the sun and the sea."

"I just want you. Naked," Daniel muttered. He gathered her to him and she felt his erection against her stomach, and felt his hand cupping her butt.

"I missed you last night," Alex told him before pushing up onto her toes and placing her lips against his. Daniel immediately responded, his tongue sliding into her mouth and sending heat to her core.

Alex, as she always did, melted and wondered if anyone would notice if they sneaked away.

"My beautiful, sexy wife. How I love—"

The door behind them banged open and Daniel cursed at the interruption. Stifling her groan, she turned to see Rachel in the hallway, Matt Galloway a step behind her. Still leaning against Daniel, she lifted her hand at her matron of honor.

Rachel rubbed her arm. "Are you okay, Alex? You're looking a bit flushed."

That was because her husband still had his hand on her butt.

"Just taking a breather," Alex told her, turning to look at Matt. "I was just telling Dan that I'm so excited to be going back to Galloway Cove for our honeymoon."

Matt nodded. "I was surprised when Dan asked me. I thought that since you were basically kidnapped and tossed off the plane onto my island, it wouldn't be your first choice for a honeymoon."

Alex shook her head. "No, I loved it!" She loved making love to Daniel at the waterfall and by the pool and on the bench, in the outdoor shower...

Rachel lifted her eyebrows at her, Alex lifted hers back and they both burst out laughing. Yep, she was pretty sure that Rachel liked the island, too. And not only because it was a place of immense natural beauty.

The door opened again, and Tessa glided through, followed by Ryan. "Alex and Rachel, there you are! I've been looking for both of you."

Alex put her back to Daniel's chest, linking her hand with the one that now rested on her stomach. Her bridesmaid looked radiant and about to burst with news. Alex held up her hand as Caleb and Shelby joined their party, followed by James and Lydia. They were just missing Brooke and Austin, but Alex had barely finished that thought when they walked into the hallway from the main entrance, Austin carrying a frame covered in brown paper.

"The gang's all here," Ryan commented.

"Alex, I want to run something by you—" James started to speak, only to be interrupted by Tessa.

"Wait, hold on, I need to—"

"Austin, honey, we need Rose and Gus," Brooke said a second later.

Alex laughed and tipped her head up to look at Daniel. He grinned down at her before lifting his fingers to his mouth to let out a shrill whistle. Their friends immediately quieted down. "We need to get back to our guests, so make it snappy." Daniel pointed to Tessa. "Tess, you're up."

"Alex, would you and Rachel both be my matrons of honor?"

Alex jumped up and down and Rachel squealed with excitement. Alex wanted to hug Tessa but Daniel held her tight. "Fantastic," he said. "Not meaning to be rude, but we need to hurry this along. I want to cut the cake, have a first dance with my bride and get to the fun part of the night."

Daniel pointed his finger at Caleb. "Go."

Shelby rested her temple on Caleb's arm. "We're having twins."

Alex let out a whoop, tore away from Daniel's hold to hug Shelby. As everyone else congratulated the happy pair, Alex took the chance to hug Tessa and then, because she was overflowing with happiness, to hug Rachel, as well.

Daniel gently hooked his finger into the back of her dress and tugged her back into her previous position. "We really do need to get back inside."

Alex nodded. "I know. Rose is going to have a fit if she finds us hanging out in the hallway with our friends."

Daniel grinned and jerked his head at James. "What's up?"

"Nothing that can't wait. I was just thinking that maybe Alex could do another fund-raising function next year."

Alex nodded enthusiastically, her mischievous side surfacing. "Absolutely. I was thinking about a skin calendar, tentatively called 'The Rogues of Royal.' I'd need you all to model. I hope you are comfortable stripping down in front of a camera."

The five male faces in front of her paled in unison. Alex looked up at her husband, who was laughing. "You know that I have no problem stripping down," he murmured before looking back at the group. "To be discussed later. Much, much later. Brooke, what have you got there, honey?"

Yet again the door opened, and Alex winced when she saw Rose's unamused face. "Ladies and gentlemen, the party is inside, not out here." This time, twelve grown men and women shuffled their feet at the displeasure in Regal Rose's voice.

Alex opened her mouth to apologize, but then her grandfather slipped past Rose, his eyes on the package in Brooke's hand. "Rosie! It's here!"

Rose clasped her hands in delight and joined Gus at Brooke's side. Alex stepped away from Daniel and wondered what was going on. "What is it?" she asked.

Rose beckoned her to come closer. The group made a circle behind them and Daniel dropped to his haunches, his hand on the frame. Alex heard movement behind Ryan and glanced over to see Hector joining the group, his eyes not moving from Daniel's face.

Gus nodded, and Daniel ripped the paper away. Alex took a moment to absorb the significance of

Brooke's painting. A wolf rested in the first of three circles—one each for her, Daniel and Jason—and beneath it, Brooke had carefully painted the words *The Silver Wolf Ranch*.

Daniel turned to look at her and she saw love and adoration in his eyes. He stood up and took her hand and raised her knuckles to his lips. "Equal partners, Slade?"

"Equal partners, Clayton," she murmured.

Daniel kept her hand in his as he led her back to their wedding reception and their guests. "One dance, the cake cutting and then I'm hauling you out of here, Lex."

Alex grinned at him. "As you already know, I'm always up for a good kidnapping, my darling."

* * * * *

A brand-new Texas Cattleman's Club miniseries begins March 2019 with
Hot Texas Nights
by USA TODAY *bestselling author Janice Maynard!*

Don't miss a single scandal!

COMING NEXT MONTH FROM

HARLEQUIN Desire

Available March 5, 2019

#2647 HOT TEXAS NIGHTS
Texas Cattleman's Club: Houston
by Janice Maynard
Ethan was Aria's protector—until he backed away from being more than friends. Now her family is pressuring her into a marriage she doesn't want. Will a fake engagement with Ethan save the day? Only if he can keep his heart out of the bargain...

#2648 BOSS
by Katy Evans
I have a new boss—and he's hot but irresponsible, a youngest son. If he thinks he can march into this office and act like he owns the place, he needs to think again... If only I didn't want him as much as I hate him...

#2649 BILLIONAIRE COUNTRY
Billionaires and Babies • by Silver James
Pregnant and running from her almost in-laws, Zoe Parker is *done* with men, even ones as sinfully sexy as billionaire music producer Tucker Tate! But Tucker can't seem to let this damsel go—is it her talent he wants, or something more?

#2650 NASHVILLE SECRETS
Sons of Country • by Sheri WhiteFeather
For her sister, Mary agrees to seduce and destroy lawyer Brandon Talbot. He is, after all, the son of the country music star who ruined their mother. But the more she gets to know him, the more she wants him...and the more she doesn't know who to believe...

#2651 SIN CITY VOWS
Sin City Secrets • by Zuri Day
Lauren Hart is trying to *escape* trouble, not start *more*. But her boss's son, Christian Breedlove, is beyond sexy and totally off-limits. Or is he? Something's simmering between them, and the lines between work and play are about to blur...

#2652 SON OF SCANDAL
Savannah Sisters • by Dani Wade
At work, Ivy Harden is the perfect assistant for CEO Paxton McLemore. No one knows that she belongs to the family that has feuded with his for generations... until one forbidden night with her boss means *everything* will be revealed!

*I have a new boss—and he's hot but irresponsible, a
youngest son. If he thinks he can march into this office
and act like he owns the place, he needs to think again…
If only I didn't want him as much as I hate him…*

Read on for a sneak peek of
Boss
by New York Times *bestselling author Katy Evans!*

My motto as a woman has always been simple: own
every room you enter. This morning, when I walk into
the offices of Cupid's Arrow, coffee in one hand and
portfolio in the other, the click of my scarlet heels on
the linoleum floor is sure to turn more than a few sleepy
heads. My employees look up from their desks with
nervous smiles. They know that on days like this I'm
raring to go.

Though it sounds bigheaded, I know my ideas are
always the best. There's a reason Cupid's Arrow swept
me up at age twenty. There's a reason I'm the head of
the department. I carry the design team entirely on my
own back, and I deserve recognition for it.

The office doors swing open to reveal Alastair
Walker—the CEO, and the one person I answer to
around here.

"How's the morning slug going, my dear Alexandra?" he asks in that British accent he hasn't quite been able to shake off, even after living in Chicago for a decade. He's adjusting his sharp suit as he saunters into the room. For his age, he's a particularly handsome man, his gray hair and the soft creases of his face doing little to steal the limelight from his tanned skin and toned body.

At the sight of him, my coworkers quickly ease back.

"The slug is moving sluggishly, you might say," I admit, smiling in greeting.

When Alastair walks in, everyone in the room stands up straighter. I'm glad my team knows how to behave themselves when the boss of the boss is around. But my own smile falters when I notice the tall, dark-haired man falling into step beside Alastair.

A young man.

A very hot man.

He's in a crisp charcoal suit, haphazardly knotted red tie and gorgeous designer shoes, with recklessly disheveled hair and scruff along his jaw.

Our gazes meet. My mouth dries up.

And it's like the whole room shifts on its axis.

I head to my private office in the back and exhale, wondering why that sexy, coddled playboy is pushing buttons I was never really aware of before. Until now.

Don't miss what happens when Kit becomes the boss!
Boss
by Katy Evans.

Available March 2019 wherever Harlequin® Desire books and ebooks are sold.

www.Harlequin.com

Want to give in to temptation with
steamy tales of irresistible desire?

Check out **Harlequin® Presents®**,
Harlequin® Desire and
Harlequin® Kimani™ Romance books!

  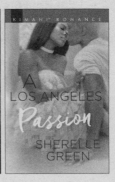

New books available every month!

CONNECT WITH US AT:

Facebook.com/groups/HarlequinConnection

Facebook.com/HarlequinBooks

Twitter.com/HarlequinBooks

Instagram.com/HarlequinBooks

Pinterest.com/HarlequinBooks

ReaderService.com

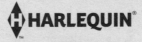

**ROMANCE WHEN
YOU NEED IT**

PGENRE2018

Love Harlequin romance?

DISCOVER.

Be the first to find out about promotions, news and exclusive content!

Facebook.com/HarlequinBooks

Twitter.com/HarlequinBooks

Instagram.com/HarlequinBooks

Pinterest.com/HarlequinBooks

ReaderService.com

EXPLORE.

Sign up for the Harlequin e-newsletter and download a free book from any series at **TryHarlequin.com.**

CONNECT.

Join our Harlequin community to share your thoughts and connect with other romance readers!
Facebook.com/groups/HarlequinConnection

**ROMANCE WHEN
YOU NEED IT**

HSOCIAL2018

THE WORLD IS BETTER WITH

Romance

Harlequin has everything from contemporary, passionate and heartwarming to suspenseful and inspirational stories.

Whatever your mood, we have a romance just for you!

Connect with us to find your next great read, special offers and more.

f /HarlequinBooks

🐦 @HarlequinBooks

www.HarlequinBlog.com

www.Harlequin.com/Newsletters

H HARLEQUIN®

A *Romance* FOR EVERY MOOD™

www.Harlequin.com